Cheryl Harness

Just
for You
to Know

HARPERCOLLINSPUBLISHERS

Library of Congress Cataloging-in-Publication Data is available.
ISBN-10: 0-06-078313-3 (trade bdg.)
ISBN-13: 978-0-06-078313-6 (trade bdg.)
ISBN-10: 0-06-078314-1 (lib. bdg.)
ISBN-13: 978-0-06-078314-3 (lib. bdg.)

1 2 3 4 5 6 7 8 9 10
❖
First Edition

For Kit, Vicki, Steph, Veda, and B.S.L.,
who listened, and for Elaine Harness, my mom

If you have built castles in the air,
your work need not be lost;
that is where they should be.
Now put the foundations under them.
—*Henry David Thoreau*

PART ONE: BEFORE

One
In which we go to our new town by way
of the graveyard, Decoration Day, May 31, 1963.

1

Two
In which we move into our new, crummy old house,
and we have company. Jimmy has his own room. I have worries.

2

Three
In which we Cathcarts and the neighbors meet each other,
Jimmy and I go to the library, and I help Mama
get out of having company.

35

Four
In which I climb a tree; I get a pen pal and a friend.
We Cathcarts go to the store.

50

Five
In which we celebrate Independence Day in Independence.
I learn more about life and death and Richie Scudder.
Robin returns and I'm so happy and then I'm not.

68

PART TWO:
AFTER

Ten
*In which Dad brings home the baby, Aunt Bevy
loses her sense of style, we have company, Velvet
and I make our acquaintance.*

Eleven
*In which I count down the oogly-boogly days until
school, Mr. Beeler has a question, the Monroe ladies have
an adventure, and maybe I have a dream, maybe not.*

Twelve
In which we go to school.

Thirteen
In which I have trouble getting my homework done.

Fourteen
*In which I fall apart in front of Andrew Jackson,
and Robin has a good idea. I look for matches.*

PART ONE: BEFORE

One

*In which we go to our new town by way
of the graveyard, Decoration Day, May 31, 1963.*

"Well, what's our address going to be?" I asked.

"715 North Cottage Avenue, Independence, Missouri, USA, Western Hemisphere, Planet Earth, third planet from the sun in the Solar System, Milky Way Galaxy, Universe," my little brother replied. Jimmy was ten years old and happy to offer information anytime, anywhere. "We're going to be at 39° north and 94° west." He pushed his glasses up with his stubby finger. "That's our longitude and latitude address, just for you to know."

As if there was a tiny **X** marking us on the world.

"No foolin'?" Dad grinned at Jimmy in the rearview mirror as he turned our old station wagon through the graveyard gate.

You know that things are pretty crummy when going to a cemetery is a high spot. We stopped, and I escaped out the car door and filled my lungs with cool green air. I filled my eyes with crooked stones, some of them topped with concrete lambs and angels, all marking long-ago funerals. Every year, no matter where we lived, we came to this old graveyard by the Missouri River and set a canning jar full of peonies by Grandma and Grandpa's tombstone.

I looked to see if there were any tears in Mama's eyes for her folks who died before I was born. There weren't. Her freckled face was mild as milk, like always. Mama was quiet as usual, and her chapped hands rested on her broad middle.

"Can they hear us up here," Clark wondered, "like reindeer on the roof on the night before Christmas?"

Now in my personal opinion, you don't exactly have to be Clark's age (seven and a half) to believe in Santa in the chimney, but did I want to imagine dead people down under the grass, listening to us, maybe jealous of us tramping around upstairs, alive in the fresh air? Nope. Still, Clark's idea sure got the twins going. Waking up the oogly-booglies in a pair of freckle-pussed six-year-olds: this is not difficult.

"What if they reached their hands up through the grass?" Larry asked Jimmy, who shrugged.

"What if they waved at us or grabbed our feet?" Harry asked me. I rolled my eyes. The twins went prancing about on tiptoe as if the cemetery were paved with hot bricks, lifting their feet high out of reach of ghostly hands. That's exactly what I want to do when I'm dead: lie in the ground waiting to scare little kids even more witless than they already are. As I traced my fingers over the carved name of a dead stranger, an idea reached out and grabbed me. It sent me hurrying back to the car for my pencil and sketchbook.

I put a sheet of paper across the face of an especially mossy old marker, one you couldn't even read. With my No. 2 pencil, I revealed a hand pointing up to the dear dead person's heavenly home. I hunted for another tombstone and found an even neater one. Biting my lower lip, I rubbed my pencil fast. A face appeared, an angel's face with eyes like headlights and bird wings on its shoulders. And then, calendar dates: November 25, 1814–April 11, 1873. A birthday and a deathday. Bookends, they seemed like, on each end of Sarah Somebody's shelf of days. I couldn't make out her real last name, the carving was so worn down. In my mind I tried to see all her sad relatives standing around this marker, this place in another springtime, all dressed in black and crying. What was she like? I imagined Sarah what's-her-name when she was alive and pale, in a long white dress. Then, on the same page, beside her pencil-rubbed angel, I slid into a daydream. I drew her long black hair, her dark eyes staring back at me from across a canyon of years, staring like the eyes of the tombstone angel when— *Smash!* Into my imaginings came grubby fingers, grabbing at my drawing, smearing the pencil, crumpling the paper. I smacked two-year-old Georgie's slobbery hand away.

"I wanted to look at it!" my littlest brother wailed.

"You messed it all up!" I shouted into his face. Georgie bawled out his hurt feelings, like he was the only one who had any. He was still blubbering as we piled back into the car, Harry and Larry scuffling like lion cubs, Dad telling me what a snot I was. "How can you be so mean over a piece of paper?"

"How come you don't yell at him for ruining my picture?"

4

"Be nice now, Carmen," Mama said.

Clark and Jimmy opened up their books, and I pressed my face against the cool window glass as our car rumbled past the rusty graveyard gate. That's when I saw an old lady off and away by the crumbliest stones in the weediest corner. Our eyes met in the instant before we were lost from each other's view. Was she there to decorate her sweetheart's grave? Maybe he had been a soldier and got killed in a war. Now there she was: a bent old lady with a jar full of lilies. Just when she's remembering their very last kiss, she sees a red-headed twelve-year-old girl staring at her out of the back of a station wagon full of kids and junky cardboard boxes. Maybe she'd think I was trying to tell her something. I imagined myself hollering, "Help! I don't belong with all these dopey little brothers! I'm being kidnapped!"

"She didn't look at all as if she belonged with them, Officer. Here, I wrote down their license number on the newspaper I wrapped around these lilies I brought for Harold." Then the police pull Dad over. "Sorry, Mister," says the cop, "but we got a report you got a kidnapped girl here."

"No, sir, we're the Cathcarts! That's my girl, Carmen,

my oldest. I'm Gene, and this is my wife, Dorothy. We just stopped here to leave off a jar of peonies."

"Is that true, little lady?" the policeman asks, narrowing his squinty eyes behind his sunglasses.

"We're the Cathcarts, all right," I say with a sigh.

He peers into the junky station wagon crammed full of Gene and Dorothy Cathcart and their six kids.

"You got my sympathy, kiddo," he says to me. . . .

"Hey!" I felt a poke in my shoulder, then Jimmy said, "I'm talking to you."

"Huh?"

"You're always daydreaming."

He's next to the oldest in our family. James Eugene Cathcart. We're both redheaded, marshmallow-middled, glasses-slipping-down-their-noses kind of kids other kids ignore. One thing at least, Jimmy's a lot squashier in the middle than I am.

"No, I'm not." Then I lied again. "I was just thinking about Blue Top." Well, not a lie exactly. I had been thinking about it—some. Anyway, Jimmy believed me.

"Remember when we stood out there and saw *Friendship Seven*?" he asked in a faraway sort of voice. "And Clark kept waving his flashlight so that astronaut—"

"John Glenn," I supplied.

"Yeah, so John Glenn could look down and see us?"

The good memory made us smile. Blue Top was where we lived, until this morning anyway, more than a hundred miles back down the road, on the other side of Osceola. Like rich people in books name their mansions, I named our crummy, weedy old farm after the meadow-topped hill there. All summer, all over, it bloomed with clover and sky-colored cornflowers. A person could lie down in them and imagine fairies in the grasses and kingdoms in the clouds. Or, lying very still, with your head pointed north and your feet to the south, you could feel the earth turn. Plus, out in the tall weeds, nobody could find you and make you come babysit or something.

Now, as one of the boys took a littler boy's toy away and they were screaming and punching each other, I said, "I guess I'll sort of miss living there."

Jimmy nodded thoughtfully. "It *was* sort of a dump."

The way he said it told me that he was proud too, partly, of our folks for doing something as nutty as buying a goat and a brushy bunch of land with a worn-out house where you had to go outside to a stinky outhouse to pee and pray that the black swooping wasps would stay outside, buzzing in the hollyhocks.

We only lived there for a year or so and, since I was little, eight different houses before that. I know because I wrote down a list. Dad said he guessed he was "just a restless sort," as if he was satisfied. He always seemed to want to be somewhere else. Me, I just wanted to be some*one* else.

We'd make new friends at our new schools, the folks always promised, but generally that wasn't true, not for Jimmy and me, anyway. I did like this one girl this past year—Janice McFarland—but I wasn't her best friend. We'll probably forget about each other now that our paths have separated. Liking the sound, I whispered out those words: *"Our paths have separated."* Mostly the girls I spent time with were ones who lived in books, like Laura Ingalls and her sisters, or those best friends in the Betsy and Tacy books. I chewed the inside of my mouth. It'd be neat to have a best friend sometime, in real life.

"Do you think that Gertie will be all right?" Jimmy asked. "Not be too lonesome over at Farmer Scott's?"

"Beats me."

Our goat, Gertie, got sold to our neighbor across the road. He was a real farmer, not like Dad who just felt like living in the country for a while, even if he did have to drive and drive and drive to get to his job in Springfield. Gertie would figure out her goat life one way or the other. Everybody had to sooner or later.

I opened up my sketchbook and smoothed out the crumpled page with imaginary Sarah and the angel rubbing. Georgie watched, real serious-like, while I used a clean corner of my eraser to get rid of the worst smudges. Just as I was trying to make Sarah's nose look prettier—it's really hard, in case you want to know, to draw the nose holes without giving the person a nose like a pig—the car hit a bump in the road. Now, on top of all her other troubles, poor Sarah had an ugly pencil mark on her lip. I blew my bangs up with an angry puff of air and looked over at Georgie.

"The car's too jiggly."

Georgie nodded. It's nerve-wracking to have paper in front of you and not be able to draw, so I held the sketchbook up so Georgie and I could look at page after smudgy page of ladies, all pretty solemn in spite of their beauty, their long hair and flowing gowns. The last page in my book was blank, like snow nobody'd walked on yet. I glided my hand across the smooth paper. The most excellent picture I'd ever draw might happen there.

A fresh thought came into my head, how white paper was like moving to a new address. Anything was possible there. What was it like, this new house? I hadn't seen it yet. All's I knew was where it was on the globe of the world and that it wasn't far from Dad's new factory job. Anyway, maybe my family and I could be different, living at 715 North Cottage.

"We're going to live pretty close to where a genuine used-to-be president of the United States lives," Dad said, looking back at all of us in the rearview mirror. "Can any of you guys tell me who that might be?"

"Harry S. Truman," I muttered. Not that people like us will ever get to see a real president out walking around, just being a guy.

"Independence was where the Oregon Trail started," Jimmy told us all. "Back in the pioneer days."

Big deal. Maybe it was an exciting place about a hundred years ago *if* you were wanting to join up with a wagon train and go on a bumpy, scary, disgusting, ox-poopy frontier trail. I could just imagine Dad saying, "Let's go to California! It'll be an adventure!"

Thank goodness we didn't have to do that.

Now Clark stabbed me in the arm with his finger. "Carmie, look at this one!" He held his joke book two inches away from my eyeballs.

"Leave me alone."

"'How do you tell if an elephant was in your refrigerator?' Do you know?" When he couldn't stand me ignoring him even one more second, he blurted out, "'When you find footprints in the Jell-O!'" Laughter exploded out of him.

The twins began fighting over graham crackers, spilling them over the checker game they were trying to play. When Harry accidentally elbowed Larry in the head, they tipped over a sack full of Mama's old magazines onto Georgie, who began to howl. Oh man, how'd I end up in Gene and Dorothy's Traveling Loony Bin? Somewhere up in heaven, I must've gotten on the wrong bus.

"You kids pipe down right now, I mean it!" Dad yelled.

"Pick up those crackers, you boys," said Mama. "And don't eat them if they've been on the floor. Throw 'em out the window for the birds and the critters."

Boy, that got their minds off their troubles: throwing all the crackers and a few checkers out the window. I hoped the rabbits or raccoons wouldn't be squashed into hash, trying to gather up smashed graham crackers all over the highway. And what would some poor hungry robin do when all he got was a checker?

"Mama!" Harry shouted. "Georgie's peeing his pants!"

"Oh gross!" Clark yelled. "Don't get any on me!"

"Carmen," said tired-sounding Mama, "you wanna change him? His red shorts are in that grocery sack."

If there was one thing I knew for sure, it was that no matter where we lived, I'd always be changing some little boy's disgusting wet pants. Once a long time ago, I changed Harry's diaper and he peed right in my eye! Clark thought this story was the funniest joke in the world. It made Harry very happy and proud.

"Let's all sing, okay?" Dad suggested. "'She'll be comin' 'round the mountain,'" he began, and even Mama and Georgie, sort of, were singing dumb stuff like "we'll all have biscuits and gravy when she comes."

"How come Carmen's not singing?" Larry asked.

Dad tossed me a glance over his shoulder. "She thinks she's too old." Then he pushed back his ball cap and began singing "I Dream of Jeannie with the Light Brown Hair" loud and deep, high-pitched Clark joining in. When the last note trailed off, Mama said, "You sang that for me the first time we ever met, when you came bumming 'round our diner, lookin' for a handout."

"Handout?" Dad retorted. "Bumming! Didn't I sing for my supper?"

I looked at the back of Dad's head and tried to see in my mind the way he was in the 1930s' hard times. Imagining my dad as a teenaged hobo, running, panting, jumping onto a moving boxcar train—it made me shiver. Maybe that was how he got to be a restless sort, being on his own after his mom died out in California. "After my daddy lost his business, he went and got drowned in the Pacific Ocean. I hit the road, saw the whole, entire US of A, I did, *and* met your mama." I didn't mind at all hearing Dad tell his story, even a million times.

Mama was working in her family's diner when her father found my tired, hollow-in-the-belly dad sleeping out back, on one of the picnic tables. Instead of telling him to "Go along and git outta here" like some people did, my grandpa said, "Go out and wash up at the pump. I'll have Dee bring you out a sandwich." Dee: that's my mom. I tried to imagine her dad, the black-and-white Grandpa in the photo album, the Grandpa in the graveyard under the peonies.

Dad smiled at Mama. "I sang to you, remember? A half a dozen songs, I bet, for two ham sandwiches and a glass of lemonade!" His open hand swirled in the hard highway wind out the driver's window. A harp with angel wings was tattooed on his sunburned arm.

"Didn't we throw in a piece of cherry pie?" Mama asked him.

"Well, your sister baked that pie. Bev's a beauty and a pistol—but a baker? No *ma'am!* And didn't I write to you, anyway? Every week, even when I went off to save the world from Hitler and the Japs and nearly got myself killed? Didn't I come home and marry you and help you make all these babies?" Dad's light eyes blazed as he waved his window arm and our old Rambler swerved there for a second, throwing all us "babies" into one another.

"Gene, you wanna be watching for a gas station?"

"You feelin' okay, honey?" Dad gave Mama a worried look.

"I'm fine."

We pulled off the blacktop into a podunk, one-pump gas station just outside our new hometown. Mom came out, and Dad was paying a blue-overalls guy for the gas when I went inside the joint. Probably the hick teenage boys hanging around the counter didn't see me go in there or else, maybe, the pimply one wouldn't have been yacking to his greasy-haired buddy about "the hill-billy family in that rust bucket out at the pump."

"The mom looks like she's got another bun in the oven," said Goop Head, lighting up a smoke.

"What a cow," Crater Face sneered. "Like they don't got enough kids already."

I stalked out of the ladies' restroom and yelled at them, "Shut up, you dopes!" Boy, I ran out of there before the surprise drained out of their stupid faces, but they pulled their sorry selves together enough to laugh at us some more as we drove away.

I met Dad's eyes in the rearview mirror. "What's the deal?" he asked.

"Nothing."

"What happened in there?" Jimmy wondered.

"Leave me alone," I muttered.

Mom aimed a questioning glance at me, then went back to window-gazing at the houses going by.

Me, I just looked down at my balled-up fists.

"Must've been something," Dad said, "the way you came tearing out of there."

Clark began practicing his reading. "'Wel-come to In-de-pen-dence, Queen City of the—' Dang! Dad! You're going too fast! I was reading the sign!"

"Of the Trails," Jimmy offered. "Trails, Clark. Because of the wagon trains."

Dad ignored them, repeated his "Must've been somethin'." I looked up from my lap to the back of Mama's head. Her hair glowed a beautiful red in the last of the sunset light. I could've stuck up for her better. Maybe said, "She is not *either* going to have another dumb baby. You don't know what you're talking about. She's just—I don't know, *big*, okay?" I could've told those jerks, "She doesn't have no stupid bun in the oven, you blockheads!"

"Are we almost there?" Larry hollered from the back of the station wagon.

"Yeah, Daddy," Harry called out from right under my feet, trying to find a checker. "We've been in this dumb car all day! Aren't we at our house yet?"

"The house is just a little ways from here now," Mama said.

"Three hours," Dad griped. "Been on the road for three hours. Is that all day?"

"Root beer!" Clark shouted. He tugged at the back of Dad's seat, pulling himself up so he could holler in his ear, "See the sign up there, Daddy? Can we get some? Can we?"

"Can't we just keep going?" I grumbled, but I was drowned out by chants of "Root beer! Root beer!"

Dad seemed to get Mom's permission. "Okeydoke, then!" he exclaimed. "Root beer, in honor of our first evening in town and . . ." We came to a stop in an empty space in the crowded drive-in. Dad gave my mom a lovey-dovey look, then reached over to bring the back of her hand to his lips. "Well," he said, "just in honor of . . . summertime."

I leaned my head out the car window. There was the night's first star, all by itself in the warm, blue twi-light. I could be that star. I could be a space traveler. If I were up there in the sky, I could appreciate this evening from far, far away. The thought orbited around and around inside my hot, tangled head.

Cars full of old couples and normal families sur-rounded the orange-and-white-painted drive-in. A cou-ple of shirtless high school boys in a pickup truck honked and yoo-hooed at the tired-looking, ponytailed wait-ress. Dad switched off the engine and flipped on the dome light so Mama could dig around in her purse and, as a bonus, everybody at the root beer stand could get a really good look at me and my messy, goofy family. I hunched my shoulders and tried to smooth my hair.

"Dad, could you turn the light off, please?" I asked politely.

"Your mom's looking for something."

"Leave it on," Clark said loudly. "I'm trying to read my joke book. Listen to this one: if a cabbage and a carrot are in a race, who wins? The cabbage. It's ahead—get it? A *head*! Oh yeah, Daddy, I wanna *big* mug."

"I like the light," said Larry, sticking his tongue out at me.

After a whole lot of noisy figuring out what everybody wanted, the twins climbed over the backseat a few dozen times, banging up against us other kids until Clark punched them and Dad started yelling. It gave them something to do while we waited for the waitress to bring her tray full of heavy, slippery mugs. Everybody in the cars beside us heard Dad smacking his lips and saying: "Man, that hits the spot, don't it?"

Georgie: "I can hold it!"

Mama: "No, let me hold your mug. You don't want to spill it, now."

Clark: "Hey, you brat, listen! I'm telling a *joke*! What do you call a . . ."

Harry: "You bumped me on purpose—Mom!"

Larry: "Daddy, he made me spill my drink!"

18

Jimmy: "Don't get any on my book!"

Mama: "Everybody be nice, now."

Dad: "All of you just put a sock in it, settle down, hurry up, and drink your drinks!" Then he turned to Mama and softened his voice. "Dee? You okay, honey?"

"What's the matter?" Jimmy asked.

Mama sighed. "I'm just—we're all tired out."

"Your mama's not feeling good," Dad said.

"Me neither," I muttered.

"Maybe Mom's gonna have another baby!" Clark hollered, as if it was the best joke yet. A mom, dad, and only child in a shiny car looked over at us Cathcarts like Mama was the old woman in the shoe.

"A baby?" Harry called out.

"Mommy's going to have a baby?" Larry shouted from the very back of the station wagon just as the waitress appeared at Dad's window to take away the tray full of mugs. She rolled her eyes, more people in the other cars chuckled, and Dad glared at all of us in his mirror. "Maybe," he said, like somebody had dared him to say it.

"Is that true?" The boys were all asking Mama, "Is that true? Are you going to really? Are you? When, Mommy? A new baby? Is that really true?"

Their flutey "trues?" and "are yous?" sounded like hooty owls. I saw Mama bow her head and Dad leaned over to kiss her cheek. "She sure is," he said, his voice all soft, his face all proud, "later on this summer."

"What?" My voice came out too angry and too loud.

Before I could stop them, hard words popped out of me like snakes out of a can. "Another dumb, stupid, bawly baby? Don't we have enough, for crying out loud?"

Dad whipped his head around in my direction. "What was that you said?"

It seemed like slow motion, but it only took a second for Dad to lunge back from the steering wheel. "You ashamed of us, Carmen? You ashamed of your own family?" His long arm whipped over the front seat, and I saw the back of his hand coming for my face.

Two

In which we move into our new, crummy old house, and we have company. Jimmy has his own room. I have worries.

I folded my arms and hated the sting in my nose: first sign of the tears that come when I'm mad. Yes, Daddy, I told him in my head, as a matter of fact, I do find our family pretty embarrassing.

He didn't slap me hard. It hurt my feelings, mostly. A bad surprise on top of a bad surprise, plus strangers and my brothers staring at me—except for Jimmy, who bit his lower lip and looked at his lap.

"You made Mama cry," Larry whispered, frowning at me. Dad tossed an "Everybody just settle down now" over the backseat and peeled out of the lot. At least everyone was quiet for a change as he drove through the dark streets. Georgie fell asleep on Mama's lap, and Clark read street signs.

"Noland Road. River Bou-le-vard. Cottage—hey! Is this our street, Daddy?" I covered my eyes with my hands, and it wasn't long before I felt us slow down, surge up a little hill, and roll to a stop on crunchy gravel.

Please, please, please, I prayed into the stillness when the engine stopped. Just don't let it be too horrible. . . . I looked to see where the latest chapter of our same old life was going to be.

Dad got out, stood up, and whooshed out a big breath of air. He pressed his hands into the small of his back and said, "Well, now!" to everybody but me, it seemed like.

"Wow," Clark breathed.

"It looks like a haunted house," Jimmy said.

We kids climbed out, me hugging my sketchbook to my chest. We all stood in the rutted driveway that ran alongside the house, which did look pretty spooky. Leafy shadows cast from the streetlight flickered across the dark windows. Even darker, inky-black treetops swayed high over the pointy roof of our tall, rickety, ratty-looking house. What would be a good name for this dump? Deep in the dark front porch, chains clinked on the swaying swing. Creepy Crappy Crummy Cathcart Castle? Across the street a light came on and, in the moment before he closed it, an old-man shape darkened a front door.

In my memory I saw our old neighborhood: a field across the road where Farmer Scott raised soybeans. Here there were sidewalks, big old houses with porches, and a streetlight on the corner, its glow lighting up a brick grade school in the next block. Clark pointed at it. "That's where us boys are going to go, except not Georgie."

"I wanna go!" Georgie whined.

Probably our house had been built and painted about the time the last wagon train rolled out of town. "A fixer-upper," Dad called it. Meaning it was either us or the wrecking ball. The spooks that lived here would probably be upstairs packing right about now and heading out to the highway to scare innocent motorists, or bunking with their relatives at the graveyard until they found a new, more peaceful place to haunt.

The air smelled like mowed lawns and purple irises. It sounded like crickets plus someone somewhere listening to a ballgame. Somebody next door was playing a piano, real good, too, with both hands. Would the folks around here be glad we moved into their neighborhood? Was there anybody in these houses who might be friends with me?

"Come on, Carmie," Dad said as he turned the key in the lock of the back door. He wasn't going to let a tight-faced twelve-year-old mess up his fresh start. Besides, once his temper flashed out a few thunderbolts, he calmed right back down again and liked everyone else to do the same.

Sorry. Not me. Too bad.

I shrunk away from Mama's hand on my shoulder, then followed everyone following Dad into the house.

The place had electricity, anyway. Light from a dim, dangling bulb shone down on our tired selves and a yellowish kitchen full of the boxes and sacks that Mom and Dad had been moving up here while I babysat everybody back at Blue Top. They were stacked here and there on the icky-looking linoleum. A mouse, probably the smartest one in her family, took one look at us and ran for her life into a crack under the cupboards.

Mama sank down on a kitchen chair and closed her hand around my wrist as I started past her. "Carmie," she said, "you and Jimmy have the two rooms up on the top floor, okay?"

"Really? My own room?" Jimmy grinned at this good surprise. It was a first for him. One good thing about being the only girl: you just about always get a room to yourself.

"Not fair!" Clark cried. He gave Jimmy an arm punch, then they scrambled for the stairs. I leaned down and pressed my cheek onto the top of Mama's head. You can be mad about having a really bad day and people not telling you things and still try to make things a little bit nice anyway.

"I'm sorry," I said, but I walked away from her before Mama could say anything back to me.

I opened one of the doors at the top of two sets of stairs. As soon as my fingers found the switch, I saw a frosted square of light fixture. The bulb in it that worked shined out as best it could through a whole bunch of moth corpses onto a slanting-down ceiling, one window, cardboard boxes, my bookcase, my bed and dresser, and brownish wallpaper all polka-dotted with clumps of oatmeal-colored lilacs.

I breathed in deep, and treated myself to *the* most satisfactory sound: the slam of a door shut tight between yourself and the whole, entire, crummy rest of the world. I flopped down on the bed and, after a moment, comforted myself by looking at my drawing of Sarah Somebody, erasing every mark that wasn't perfect. I scrubbed my pencil back and forth, sharpening it on the cardboard back of the sketchbook, and drew curving lines around her face. Press softly, then harder: thin then thick then thin again. My pencil gave her graceful curls and made me feel calm until—*tap, tap, tap*.

Jimmy's voice followed the *taps* through the wall: "I've never had my own room before. This is so neat! Carmen, how come you're so mean about the new baby?"

Before I could answer, which I wasn't going to, the far-downstairs sounds of a noisy kid chorus announced company at the front door and a foghorn voice cried out, "I can only stay a minute!"

"Aunt Bevy's here!" Jimmy cried. He and I got downstairs just as Mom was coming out of the kitchen and saying to herself, "Oh, for crying out loud." She loved her big sister, but did she like unexpected company? Not at all.

"Say, Bev, comin' to see us on a Friday night?" Dad teased. "Seems like you'd be out on a date."

26

Aunt Bevy's bright lips tightened before she replied, "So I am—with you guys!" So I figured she must've gotten her heart busted again. Our only aunt lived over in Kansas City with a poodle named Trixie and no husband, "but not for want of trying," said Daddy. Aunt Bevy told me once about her long-ago husband, Bill. "He got shot in the big war by some Nazi son-of-a-gun." She'd been on lots of dates. "But nobody was ever as nice as Bill." Aunt Bevy worked in the hat department at a big store downtown where people called her "Miss Gillespie." She was what Dad called a "career gal."

Tonight Aunt Bevy swept into our front room in her turquoise pedal pusher outfit. She'd stabbed chopsticks into the top of her dark brown, ratted-up, swept-up hairdo. As she hugged Mama to her perfumed, smoky-smelling self, I couldn't help thinking that my mom sure was the opposite of her skinny, stylish sister. In her homemade pastel dresses, Mama was like a candy-colored cloud. She was quiet like a cloud too, big and puffy soft with thunder hidden inside.

"Might I offer you ladies a swig of Kool-Aid?" Dad asked them.

When everyone took him up on his offer, I got up to help. "No, now, Buddy," Dad told me, "I can manage."

Buddy's my nickname. It meant Dad was sorry for popping me in public.

Mama smiled at him and plopped in her rocking chair by the bay window. Aunt Bevy gave us kids hugs of our own, saying, "Be an angel, Jimmy-pie, and bring me an ashtray, will ya, please? Now which one of you twins is Larry? Say there, Georgie-boy! You been takin' cute pills? Clark, knock-knock!"

A big grin split Clark's skinny face. "Who's there?"

"Boo," Aunt Bevy replied, firing up one of her stinky Lucky Strikes. She smiled when Clark answered back, "Boo who—oh man, everybody knows that one!"

"Whatcha cryin' for!" Harry shouted, really happy to supply the punch line.

Aunt Bevy gave me the usual "Carmen, look how tall you've gotten!" But she made up for it, digging a sack out of her huge straw purse and handing it to me.

"Hey, thanks," I said, pulling out a fresh pad of drawing paper, "I really needed this!"

"Good goin', Bev," Dad drawled. "That's the first smile anyone's gotten out of Carmen all day." I ignored him and followed Aunt Bevy's gaze around our jumbled front room. She frowned up at our chandelier. "It looks just the tiniest bit like a flying saucer, wouldn't you say?"

"I think it looks more like that Russian satellite," said Jimmy. "You know: *Sputnik*." To me it was more like a garbage can lid fitted out with lightbulbs, but I wasn't going to say so. Its puny glow lit up the ceiling's water stains. I searched them for shapes and faces, like you would in clouds.

Aunt Bevy, who'd gone back to searching through her big purse, cried, "Ta-da!" and whipped out a—well, it looked like a wad of soda straws. Then she jumped to her feet and sort of let go of the straws, but they didn't spill all over the place like you'd think because they were all tied together with thread in a way that turned the straws into corners, angles, and towers.

"A straw castle!" she exclaimed, ignoring Georgie playing piano on her Calypso Coral toenails. She didn't seem to notice Larry tugging her shirt as she hung her present from the bottom of our *Sputnik* chandelier. She grinned down at Mama. "Remember how Pop used to always have one of these in the diner?"

"Auntie Bevy?" said Larry.

"He called it his dream castle in the air," Mama said.

I repeated the words to myself: *dream castle in the air.* Neat.

Larry spoke louder. "Aunt Be-VY!"

"Honey, your mother and I were—"

"Guess what?" Blabbermouth Harry interrupted Aunt Bevy and spilled all the beans. "Mommy's gonna have another baby, didja know that?"

"Hey!" Larry shouted. "I was gonna tell her!"

"Ha-ha, I beat you!"

"Brat!"

"Stupid!"

"You two pipe down!" Dad said, picking his way across the room, pitcher in one hand, sack of Dixie cups in the other. He shot me a sharp look, like he was double-dog-daring me to say something about the baby.

"A baby?" Aunt Bevy's skinny drawn-on eyebrows frowned low in Dad's direction. They shot right back up again as she tilted her head and flashed her eyes over at my mom.

So. I wasn't the only one who didn't think a new baby was such hot news.

Aunt Bevy bent down to kiss my mom's cherry-colored cheek. Mom's hands rested on her big stomach, sort of like she was protecting it, and her eyes seemed to be telling her big sister to mind her own business. If Aunt Bevy had any worries or questions, she hid them. She squeezed my mom's hand and lied like she was supposed to.

"I think it's just wonderful, Dee-dee. 'Bout time for a little girl, don't you expect? I think I know someone who could use a sister 'round here." Aunt Bevy smiled at me. "Help you out with all these brothers, huh, Carmenita?"

A sister? Helping me?

"Sometime in the fall, right?" Aunt Bevy asked, fiddling with her silver cigarette box.

Mama flickered a smile in Dad's direction before saying, "Probably sooner." Aunt Bevy was getting ready to set fire to another one of her Lucky Strikes, then she glanced at Mama and decided to take a tiny sip of orange Kool-Aid instead. She wrinkled her powdered nose.

Clark pointed at Mom's midsection. "Is it moving around in there?"

"What?" the twins demanded.

"The new baby! Scooch over!" Clark told Georgie.

Soon all four of the little boys were crowding in to mash their heads up against Mama's belly like bandits listening to railroad tracks to hear if a train was coming. I went over and gave Aunt Bevy a good night-and-good-bye hug. "Thank you again for the sketchbook."

I made my escape upstairs and put a closed door between me and my family. I leaned against it, listening to their distant voices. As my eyes got used to the dark, as the storm clouds inside of me smoothed out, I walked over to the window. What I saw made me smile. I was up so high, like I was in a tower room in a fairy tale castle, like in the story of Rapunzel, except my hair wasn't long enough for anyone to come up and get me.

I beat on the window frame until it opened, looked past and through the dark treetop to the yards and street way down below. Dad and some of the boys were walking Aunt Bevy to her Volkswagen Beetle. I could just barely hear Dad telling her, "You be safe now." It wasn't hard to hear Aunt Bevy's loud voice: "It'll be mighty nice to have you all close by. Is Carmen okay? She seemed kind of grumpy and out of sorts."

I tried to hear what Dad said to her, but all I got was a bunch of "nighty-nights" before my aunt's car rumbled away. The sounds of doors closing, kid voices, and stair stomping sifted through the house.

"'Grumpy and out of sorts,'" I muttered. I folded

my arms on the windowsill and rested my chin on them.

Another baby. *Seven* children. Maybe a big family would be all right if you were rich and famous like President Kennedy and all of his brothers and sisters. But . . . I thought about those gas station jerks and people staring at us like weren't they lucky not to be like us messy, ugly, noisy, stupid Cathcarts.

Oh, sometimes I hated every single feeling in my head! They all came running out like roaches when you turned on the light in the kitchen. I should have had a can of thought spray.

I sat down on a box full of books, smoothed my hand across my new drawing pad, and thought about my parents. They loved babies. I just had to face it. For them babies were like a clean sheet of paper or a new address: a fresh start, everything possible, and nothing ruined yet. Sort of like a first day of school, which was another terrible thing to be gloomy and nervous about: a new school, probably a thousand times bigger than our school back in Vista. And this wasn't even going to be plain old elementary—this would be junior high!

Oh, put a sock in it. Don't be a crabby pouty-baby over things you can't stop from happening. Then a woman's voice interrupted the mean lecture I was giving myself.

"Ro-bin," she called, "for heaven's sake come down out of there. It's past your bedtime!"

A chubby-looking girl emerged out of the pool of shadow at the bottom of the big tree in the neighbors' yard! She looked right up at my window and waved at me! Then she stomped up her front steps and went inside without even looking to see if I waved back.

Three

In which we Cathcarts and the neighbors meet each other,
Jimmy and I go to the library, and I help Mama
get out of having company.

It was still dark early morning when Dad put his freshly
shaved and Aqua Velva'd face close to mine and asked,
"Are we still buddies?"

"Sure."

"You try and get along with your mama today,
okay?" I felt a kiss and his warm peppermint breath on
my cheek. "She's gonna need your help this summer.
No spending all your time with your nose in a book or
drawing pictures. You're a big girl now."

"Okay," I told him. Okay, okay, just go away. Then,
to make up for thinking that, I wished him good luck

on his new job. He wasn't a mean dad, not really.

I found Mama in the basement, stuffing jeans into her washing machine. We didn't have one at Blue Top. There she had to wait until Daddy could drive her to the Washeteria in Osceola. She pointed at a couple of big laundry baskets. "The best way to help me," she said, "would be to go hang all this on the line out back. How 'bout that?"

"Okay." I couldn't help noticing that she sort of leaned against the washer, as if she was too pooped to stand on her own. "But don't you wanna go up and lay down or something?"

"It's nice and cool down here. I'll be up in a minute, and later," she said, "maybe you and Jimmy might want to take a walk? See the neighborhood? Not too far, you understand, but maybe you could get acquainted with the library up on the town square? I think it's on Liberty Street. We don't have to get all settled right today, do we?"

"Nope," I said. "We could put it off a day or two." I returned her smile, then I about killed myself, lugging first one heavy basket of wet clothes, then another up the steps and out the back door. I got a look at our new old house in the daytime. It looked better at night, I

36

decided, and pretty ratty compared to all the other houses on our street. As I pinned up two or three hundred underpants and things, Clark and the twins played hide-and-seek among the wet work pants and bedsheets with a goofy-looking kid with a blond flattop. "This is Darren Culpepper from next door," said Clark. "This is Carmen. She's the oldest."

The little squirt didn't seem to know what to say to that. He just wiped his nose with the back of his hand and squinted up at me so I asked him, "You any relation to somebody called Robin?"

"She's my big sister."

"You guys got a tree house in your front yard?"

The kid frowned. "Yeah, but Robin hardly ever lets me play in it."

As soon as Jimmy and I started out on our walk, the old man across the street waved at us and began shuffling across his tidy yard. "Hello there!"

The old fellow offered us the hand he wasn't using on his cane. We shook it and smiled back at him. "Let me tell you children, Welcome to the neighborhood," he said. "I'm Oscar Herman. Isn't that a terrible name: Oscar?"

"I kind of like it," Jimmy said.

"Me too," I added, and it was true.

"She's Carmen Cathcart, and I'm Jimmy. I'm her brother."

"Why, those are nice names!" said Mr. Herman with a grin. His teeth looked very white and store-bought. "Happy to know you." Now he used his free hand to tip his ball cap at us. He pointed his walking stick up the street to where two straw-hatted black ladies were bent over working in a garden full of zinnias.

"They'd be the Monroe sisters." Mr. Herman cranked his voice up louder, "Hey there, Miss Lillian. Pretty day, Miss Effie!"

They waved and called out, "Mornin', Oscar."

"These here're your new neighbors, Carmen and Jimmy!" He paused a little bit and hollered, "Cathcart!" We all waved and said "Hey" to each other.

Mr. Herman said to us, softly now, "Miss Effie's the skinny one, and the fat one's Miss Lillian. They both got the arthur-itis—so do I!—but they sure do keep up their flowers."

"Sir," I told him, "we gotta go to the library. Can we bring you a book?"

His furry eyebrows rose up at the suggestion. "No

thanks, I got forty chapters to go on the one I'm readin'."
He told us how to find the library as he reached into his
pants pocket for a couple of thick white peppermints.

"You and Jimmy take these now."

We thanked him and headed up the sidewalk. It
was shaded by trees, broken and humped in places from
their roots, like toes poking up under the blankets.
Jimmy's T-shirt was stretched over his soft middle and
tucked into his corduroys. I had on my cutoffs. They
showed off my knobby white legs to anyone who might
be watching. Up by the house on the corner, someone was.

"Hey, Jelly-Belly! Who's your bird-legged girl-
friend?" A high school kid sneered and blew a puff of
cigarette smoke at us. He was leaning on the propped-
open hood of a big car, the kind my dad called a "road
barge." It sat next to a rusty-looking pickup truck. "You
part of that hillbilly family that moved into the spook
house?"

He looked like he'd put the black oil from his old
Cadillac right on his hair. Just as this bozo flicked his
cigarette at us, a flying something out of nowhere
bopped him on the head. "Ow!" he yelped.

There she was, the moon-faced tree girl, standing

in the middle of the sidewalk with her hands on her hips. "That's what you get, Richie Scudder, you creep!"

"Yeah, yeah, big talk, Pudge," he jeered back. He picked up the apple she'd thrown at him and took a bite out of it. "I was just welcoming the little twerps to the neighborhood."

The girl spit on the sidewalk in his direction, then walked over to us.

"Richie thinks being a bully makes up for being a dope."

She was pretty. Her eyes were the kind with smoke rings around the blue, and her skin was pale like Snow White, who'd have gotten terrible sunburns if she hadn't lived with dwarves in the woods where it was shady. I admired the red ribbons braided through her long black pigtails and couldn't help grinning at her.

"You're Robin Culpepper, right?"

She frowned, me knowing her name and all. "So who are you?"

"Carmen Cathcart."

Jimmy poked his hand out at her the way Mr. Herman had to us. "And I'm James."

James?

Robin smiled and shook his hand.

"You want to come with us?" he asked. "We're going to get our library cards." She tilted her head sideways, sizing us up. "I gotta go ask."

At first I was afraid she'd be sorry she went to all the trouble of getting her folks to let her go for a walk with us because Jimmy was in an informative mood. He told her all the other kids' names, that we'd lived on a farm, that we used to have a goat named Gertie, and that goats' eyes are shaped like rectangles.

"Not the whole eye, but the black pupil thing in the middle. Our eyes and turtle eyes are round— cats' are pointy. That's just for you to know. And guess what else?" he said before I could shut him up. "Our mom's gonna have another baby!"

"Neato! A brand-new baby—right next door! It must be fun, being in a big family," Robin said, digging a yo-yo out of her shorts pocket. "Ours is just my folks and Darren and me."

Fun? The words "hillbilly family" were still scorched and smoking in my brain. I glanced at Jimmy and said, "It's sort of fun. Sometimes." Okay, it was.

Sometimes.

Richie came roaring past us, blasting his car horn. "Creep!" we called after him.

"It's a good thing you guys moved into that house," Robin said, sending her yo-yo out and back, *snap.* "I was afraid it was gonna be buried in weeds and junk like a Sleeping Beauty castle with the ghost of Old Lady Millinder—that used to be her house, you know—still spooking around in there. Or it'd get torn down like my mom says it should've been years ago—" Robin flicked a wary look at us. "Sorry. I shouldn't have talked about your house like that."

Since I didn't want to say I agreed with her mom, I changed the subject. "So is your junior high school really big?"

Robin yo-yoed a few steps before she said, "Yeah. When I first went there last year, in seventh grade, I got lost a lot. You gotta be quick between classes, getting to your locker and stuff."

Oh brother.

"We'll walk by Maple Street," she went on, "so you can see it if you want to."

"I do," said Jimmy.

The brick school building looked old-fashioned—and huge, compared to the school we'd been going to. Jimmy and I stared at it while Robin rocked the baby with her yo-yo. I think she figured out I was nervous.

"'Everybody's dumb the first week' is what my dad says, and he teaches high school." Then Robin kind of bugged out her eyes. "This whole junior high thing gives me the creeps. Don't tell anyone, but I still miss elementary."

"Me too," I said, feeling relieved. Maybe eighth grade wouldn't be too gross after all. To make myself seem like a casual person someone would want to be friends with, I picked up a stick and clattered it along a picket fence as we went on walking. "Have you always lived in this town?"

Robin nodded. "Same old house, same old town. Boring, huh?"

"I think that'd be neat," I said softly.

"Me too," said Jimmy.

"Hey," Robin said, "if you guys are new, maybe you don't know that big white house over there is where President Truman lives, him and his wife."

"He's the one who decided to drop the big bombs on Japan," Jimmy told us, even though we knew that already, of course. "Dad said it settled their hash once and for all and ended World War II, but still. . . . Do you guys suppose he has nightmares? About those bombs?"

Robin didn't think so, but she didn't look too sure about it. "Do you like President Kennedy?" I asked, following after her.

"My dad and I do. My mom voted for Mr. Nixon, though."

I liked our president. I'd tried to draw him and the First Lady a thousand times, but I never yet made them look as handsome and beautiful as they did in Mama's magazines.

We walked past a statue of Andrew Jackson on a prancing horse on a big stone pedestal. Robin gave Jimmy a poke in the arm. "They named this county here after him. Just for you to know."

Jimmy gazed up at the statue. "He was the seventh president," he said, kind of automatic and dreamy. Robin's eyebrows went up, like she'd never met anybody like my brother.

In the dim, cool library, Robin aimed us at a lady who gave Jimmy and me library card forms to fill out. "You can each check out one book today," she said, "since this is your first visit."

"Do you have any art books?" I asked.

It turned out that she had loads of big, thick, glossy ones. Robin and Jimmy went off to the kids books

44

while I followed the librarian's pointed finger to the art section. "Boy," I whispered, "I'm going to love living here!"

I pulled a heavy book out of a bottom shelf. The outside said *Botticelli*. That was the painter's last name, it turned out. The book was full of pictures of what must have been his painted daydreams of a mythological country full of pale, purely beautiful goddesses with long necks like flower stems.

Just the sort of fairy tale perfection you'd never find in real life. Not in mine, anyway.

"You gonna carry that book all the way home?" Robin asked. "It must weigh four or five tons."

"It's okay." I cradled the book in my arms, which were about to fall off by the time we got to the grade school on the corner by our street.

"That school's about three times bigger than the school we went to in Vista," said Jimmy.

"My mom teaches first grade there," said Robin. "Hey, maybe she'll have your little brothers in her class."

I rolled my eyes. "Lucky her."

Robin glanced at her house. "You guys wanna come in?"

"Uh, no thanks." Jimmy held up his biography of

Kit Carson from the library. "I gotta go read my book."

"I do," I told him, "so could you take this with you?"

"Sure, okay." Jimmy took my Botticelli book, then made a face like I'd handed him a sack of cannonballs.

Robin's house smelled like Clorox, Ajax, furniture polish, floor wax, and cake-in-the-oven. I marveled at the tidy, polished, rich-people living room. There was even a shiny black piano with its lid up, like on television. I saw a bit of gleaming kitchen.

"My folks must be in the backyard or something," said Robin. "Wanna come see my room?"

"Sure!" All along the carpet-covered stairway, pictures of Darren and Robin, from baby days to now, marched up the walls. At the top of the stairs, there were suitcases.

"We're going up to Minnesota to visit my grandparents," Robin said, seeing my curiosity. "We go every year."

We just met and she was leaving? That was a lousy thing to find out. "When will you be back?"

"After the Fourth of July," she said. "This is my room."

It was like walking into a magazine picture of "A Perfect Blue and White Bedroom for Your Little Girl."

There was a dollhouse in the corner, and a canopy over Robin's bed. It made me feel kind of crummy and jealous.

"Where have you been?"

A tall woman with short dark hair and a starched blouse was standing in the doorway. It looked like you could slice boiled potatoes with the sharp crease in her slacks.

"We went to the library, Mom. Dad said I could go—"

"Well then, you can tell him why you're late for your piano lesson. Did you go downtown with your blouse not even ironed?" Then she looked at me and flicked the smile switch in her head to ON. "I'm Mrs. Culpepper, Robin's mother. And you're—?"

"Carmen Cathcart," I said. "Uh . . . we just moved here yesterday. You know, next door." I motioned my hand in the direction of my house while Robin tried to iron her plaid blouse with her fingers.

"Well, Carmen," Mrs. Culpepper said as we followed her down the steps past all the pictures, "your mother must have her hands full, getting settled and all. And is it true what my son tells me? That she's going to have another little one soon?"

"Yes, ma'am." My face felt like one of those cartoon thermometers going hotter, up, up, up.

Aunt Bevy said once, "For every person you meet, there's a wonderful-horrible set of stories that would just flat wear you out if you knew 'em." Just by going in her house and meeting her mom, I got a lot of clues about Robin. I decided that Mrs. Culpepper probably deserved to have Harry and Larry in her class.

"Is this the girl next door?" said a deep voice. The light-haired, cheerful guy who owned it gave Robin's braid a friendly tug. "Jim Culpepper," he said, sticking out his hand for a shake.

"I'm Carmen, uh, Carmen Cathcart. Nice to meet you."

Robin's mom went off to her shiny kitchen. Mr. Culpepper plunked himself down at the piano and began playing as good as on a record. He asked me if I liked Beethoven, and I wondered if maybe he taught music at the high school.

"Uh, yes, sir. I think so."

"Caaaaaar-men," Clark hollered from out in the yard, "Mama wants you!" just as Robin's mom appeared beside me, a cake in her hands.

"We'll walk over with you, Carmen, and welcome

48

your mother to the neighborhood—Jim?" She'd have snapped her fingers at him, seemed like, if she hadn't had her hands full. I looked from Robin to her parents. Good grief! These tidy people? In our crummy old messy house?

"No!" I blurted.

Four

*In which I climb a tree; I get a pen pal
and a friend. We Cathcarts go to the store.*

Mrs. Culpepper's mouth opened and her eyebrows shot
up to her teeny bangs. "I beg your pardon?"

"Uh, my—I mean, no thank you, ma'am. That's real
nice about the cake," I babbled my way out the door.
"But, well—we're allergic! And I gotta go home now.
Nice to meet you guys—honest!"

Outside, goony Darren and Clark were yelling, "So
long!" to each other and "Hi!" to Dad as our old Rambler
surged up the driveway. Harry and Larry exploded out
the front door. "Daddy's home!" Dad's eyes and big grin
looked light in his grimy face. He wiped his hand on his

work pants and handed me his lunchbox so he could hug my shoulder. "Hey, Buddy. How's your mom?"

"She's fine." Especially now, I thought, since I'd saved her from what we both hated: snooty company just showing up and dropping in. "Did your job go okay?"

"Well, if you don't mind getting bossed around, being on your feet all day, lugging loads, and turning screws, it was all right. Beats lookin' for a job!" He stopped paying attention to me so he could pick up the twins. They clung to him like baby monkeys as we all went up the porch steps, Dad hollering, "Dor-thy!"

Next door Robin was making a silly face at me and twirling her finger at the side of her head. I frowned back at her. Did she mean me or her cranky mom? I went on inside.

Robin probably meant I was the nutty one, saying we were allergic to cake and running off like that. But then I looked around and saw what Mrs. Culpepper would have seen, through her ice-cube eyes.

We'd only been here one day, and already George had scribbled on the walls. Toy trucks, squashed gobs of clay, Tinkertoys, and blocks covered the floor. I saw baskets of clothes waiting to get folded, cereal bowls, and chocolate milk glasses perched on stacks of Mama's beloved magazines. I saw a roach speeding home to the wife and kids living in a 1957 *Ladies' Home Journal.* The little boys had crowded back around the television, their faces six inches from the black-and-white blast of *Three Stooges* reruns. Jimmy was flopped on our squashy couch with the poking-out springs and falling-out stuffing. He was eating a sandwich and reading about Kit Carson, using my art book for a lap desk. I sniffed at peanut butter, grubby boys, and . . . something else.

As soon as I got my art book stowed under my pillow upstairs, I clumped back down to find Georgie. "Come on, kid," I said. "Let's go find you some dry pants, okay?"

He smiled up at me. "Okay, Carmie."

"You gonna remember to go potty like a big boy next time?"

His smile dimmed. "Okay."

Robin would be cuckoo too, if she was always having to get some little squirt to use the bathroom like regular people.

I peeled wet training pants down Georgie's rubbery legs as he held tight to my shoulders. I imagined how I'd transform my house and everybody in it. I dug around, searching for a little pair of dry pants, and decided I wouldn't be cheerful about making us Cathcarts perfect. I would not whistle while I worked, like Snow White did in the cartoon. I wouldn't sweet-talk bunnies and birdies into helping me. No, I'd be a goddess, a fierce one. I saw, like a movie in my mind, my white robes, my long red hair flowing and blowing against the blackest of thunderclouds. Sparks shot out of my keen (no glasses) mythological eyes. With a well-aimed lightning bolt, *clean* became our house! *Out* went the television reception right in the middle of the boys' cartoons—*zap!* Into a giant trash can would go all our junk: everything but the encyclopedia and whatever was mine. How the flames would lick the clouds!

In real life Daddy was smooching Mama, all blushes and giggles. He even kissed her butter-yellow dress where it was stretched over her belly and the baby inside. I felt my own face get hot.

I survived all of the usual suppertime burps, farts, spills, sit-up-straights, clean-your-plates, and don't-play-with-your-foods, only to see Darren Culpepper's face mashed into the front door screen. "Clark! You in there? Come get this cake, wouldja? My mom made it for you guys. Then can you come out and play?"

Robin was out there too. I hurried out to the porch,

telling her, "It's so nice and cool out here. You wanna sit on the swing?"

She did, all the time stealing glances through the window, trying to see what was so mysterious in our house that I wasn't asking her to come in like any regular person with nice manners would do. Robin seemed to be wondering exactly what kind of a goon I was. "How come you didn't want us to come over? And you were fibbing, right? About cake making you guys sick?"

"Well, uhm, we aren't really settled yet and, you know, company makes my mom nervous. . . ." She looked at me like lawyers on TV look at criminals in the witness chair.

"Okay, okay," I said. "I just didn't want you all to find out that we're a bunch of nuts."

"You did seem pretty crazy. Of course, I like that in a person. My mom just said that she wished I was allergic to cake so I wouldn't be so fat."

"She did?"

Instead of answering, Robin pointed at the tree in her yard. "You wanna come and see my office?"

"Sure." I really did, too, but I got scared as soon as she was up there and I was still on the safe, hard ground.

She called down through the leaves, "Come on! You're not a scaredy-cat, are you?"

I was. I was a nut *and* a scaredy-cat.

I struggled up the rope ladder until Robin helped me onto the floorboards that had been wedged into three big branches. The leafy roof made deep shadows, so she shone her flashlight on an old sofa cushion and a wooden box with a lid and a lock. "To keep Darren and the other squirrels out," Robin said. It was stocked with a half-eaten bag of potato chips, pencils, a notebook, some jacks, acorns, a spare yo-yo, two candy bars, and a package of pink Hostess Sno Balls. She ripped these open, handed me one, and took one for herself. I fished a Trixie Belden mystery out of the box. "You read these too?"

"Yeah, Nancy Drew, Sue Barton, Betsy-Tacy, Laura and Mary on the prairie. I like all those books."

"Me too."

"This is the best part of my whole life," Robin said. She popped half a Sno Ball into her mouth all at once. She ate the other half, licked her fingers, flicked a cake crumb down at her house, and said, "Mom doesn't allow me to eat junk like this."

We swatted at mosquitoes and dangled our legs off

the edge of the tree house in the blue-green twilight. It smelled like summer. I could see Mama moving about in the yellow light of our kitchen. It was quiet around us except for birds and crickets until we both heard Mrs. Culpepper crabbing around inside her house. "She sounds kind of mad," I said, and hoped that wasn't rude.

Robin snorted. "Old Yeller. My mom's got a nickname, and she doesn't even know it."

I put a hand over my smile.

"She's okay, really," said Robin. "She likes everything just so and wishes I weren't such a big fat tomboy and was cute and precious like Darren. My dad doesn't yell at us. He's nice. So tell me about your folks."

When I hesitated, Robin said, "It's not a pop quiz, you know."

"Well, my mom's pretty quiet and my dad's nice too, except for when he gets mad. He blew his top the other night and smacked me."

"Huh?"

I felt guilty, tattling on my basically good dad, but I did it anyway. "He did. Right in front of half the town over at Mugs Up."

"He did not!"

"Did."

"Why?" Like I must've done something terrible.

"I shot my mouth off about Mom having another baby."

"Don't you like being in a big family?"

If I said no, I'd be a traitor, plus it wouldn't be exactly true. And it'd sound too dumb to say I'd rather be an artist than a big sister. After a long moment of me not knowing what to say, Robin handed me a Milky Way and punched me in the arm, friendly-like. A girl never did that before, and it gave me a nice feeling. I punched her arm too and unwrapped the candy.

"I wish you guys didn't have to go to Minnesota." And I wished we could just stay up in the tree forever, but no. We jumped at the sound of Mrs. Culpepper saying, "You and Carmen had better come on down out of there. It's late."

"In a minute," Robin called down.

"Now!" her mom barked. "I've got your bathwater running." She disappeared with a soft *thwack* of the screen door.

It was late, late, late before I fell asleep. The pictures

57

in the Botticelli book from the library were too beautiful to stop looking at. I ran my fingers over the perfect faces Mr. Botticelli painted. Was that how Italian ladies looked in the 1400s? If I really practiced, could I draw and paint like that? Be a great American artist in the 1900s? The thought made a buzzing by my heart.

The book was beside me in my bed when I woke up. I looked out the window and saw that the Culpeppers' shiny black Buick was gone. It was off somewhere, carrying them north to Minnesota.

Clark yelled at me from way downstairs. "Car-mie! Robin left a note for you! Under the front door! Want me to read it to you?"

"NO!" I scrambled into my shorts. I ran downstairs while Clark bellowed, "'Dear Carmen, I'm real glad you guys moved next door—'"

"Stop it, you little brat!"

"'We could be pen pals if you want,'" he went right on. "'Here's my grandma's address—'"

I grabbed the letter away from my dopey brother. He laughed, then a lightbulb must've lit up in his pointy little head. "So then could I write to Darren?"

"If you *can* write," I muttered, reading over the note for myself. I smiled: Robin Culpepper wanted us to write to each other.

"As good as you," he told me, and stuck out his tongue. It had crumbs on it, plus there was chocolate frosting all around his mouth from having Mrs. Culpepper's cake for breakfast. We all did and saved the last slice for Dad.

"Robin's mom is kind of cranky," I said to Mom, "but she sure makes good cake."

"We'll write her a thank-you note."

"I've got the address. Robin and me are pen pals."

When I wrote to her, I tried to make babysitting little brothers, hanging laundry on the clothesline, and making Kool-Aid sound super-interesting. I didn't tell her about the best part of my life: staring at the Botticelli pictures and trying to draw my favorites, in case she might think I was a goon. And I was too shy or maybe too chicken to tell Robin I missed her, but she was brave. On the back of a fish postcard she wrote,

Dear Carmen,
My grandpa took me to this lake. I caught a walleye. To see what it looks like, turn this card

over. Are you guys getting settled? Tell James
I say hello. Yours till the ocean wears rubber
pants to keep its bottom dry.

Your friend,
Robin Delaine Culpepper
P. S. I miss talking with you.

I couldn't help smiling with happiness; then I
chewed my lower lip. Robin hadn't been inside our
house yet. Would she want to be my friend if she ever
saw how messy we were and that we *never* get settled?
She might think we're lazy bums instead of just folks
who couldn't ever seem to get organized. We never
found enough places to put stuff away and, no matter
how junky, our old clothes and magazines were, according to Mama, "too good to throw away." We piled it all
in corners and shoved it under beds.

"I'll sort through it all one of these days," Mom
said, settling herself on the couch in front of the fan.
"Georgie, come take a nap with Mama."

"No."

Almost two whole weeks after we moved in, I found
our guardian angel picture in a paper sack and put it up

in the front room. It'd hung on the wall at Blue Top and every other place we'd lived. The angel wasn't as beautiful as Mr. Botticelli would have painted her, but she was okay. A hundred times I'd tried drawing her floaty hair and soft face. She was always on duty, keeping a pair of pink-cheeked little knuckleheads from falling into a bright blue river. How did angels get their robes off over their wings, I wondered. And did they ever get tired of having to watch over people?

I asked Mama, "Do you think we really have a guardian angel?"

She opened her eyes and looked at the ceiling, as if our angel might be gazing back at her through the cloudy water stains. "Oh," she said, in her soft, vague-sounding voice. "I'm pretty sure we do."

On a postcard with a picture of a wagon train on it, I wrote to Robin about it.

Saturday, June 14, 1963

Dear Robin,

Do you believe in guardian angels? I think I do. I saw the baby kick from inside my mom. Her belly feels like a basketball. It's kind of

creepy imagining that somebody's <u>inside</u> of
there, thinking about stuff. What if <u>this</u> baby
is twins, like another Harry and Larry?
Scary! It's boring here without you next door.
I miss you too.

When you're old and you have twins
(I hope you won't!),

Don't come to me for safety pins.

Mama walked by me as I was writing, "Your Friend,
Carmen."

"Carmie, don't let me forget my pickles and sardines when Daddy takes us to the store later."

I grimaced at (1) the treats Mama loved to eat when
she was going to have a baby and (2) us Cathcarts going
to the store together.

"Oh, the kids and I will go in for you, Dee," Daddy
said, later that evening. "You rest yourself out here in
the car. Just gimme your list, why doncha?"

"No, now, I'm fine," Mama told him. "I like to pick
things out."

Would it even do any good to ask to stay in the station wagon by myself and draw? Or try, in the store, to

62

keep my distance from my slow-moving mom and the rest of my family? Nope.

Dad grabbed a cart and patted Mama's arm. "Carmie and I will keep the boys out of your hair."

Looking after little kids mostly boils down to following them around, trying to keep them from getting broken while they're breaking everything else. Now they were sliding down the slick floors between rows of canned goods. That's where Harry dropped a can of peaches in heavy syrup on his foot; then Dad gave Larry a spanking for horsing around and busting a box of eggs.

Both twins were bawling when a woman on the loudspeaker barked, "Cleanup in Aisle 8." I was keeping my eyes down, or I would have noticed that the kid with the paper hat and the mop was none other than creepy Richie Scudder. "Oh man, I might've known," he said, real loud so people would know how disgusting and messy we Cathcarts were. An annoyed-looking woman and the cutest boy I ever saw turned to stare at us. And wouldn't you know, they were right next to us later on, over in Aisle 3: Paper Products and Hygiene Items, where Clark was practicing his reading.

"Carmen," he hollered. "What the heck are 'sa-ni-tar-y nap-kins'?"

The cute, sandy-haired boy made a face, and his mom rolled her eyes like we were the world's worst, low-class weirdos.

Could there *be* anything more embarrassing?

"Carmie," Dad called to me as I fled the scene, "you're as red as a tomato! There's nothing to be shy about!" Which made the whole thing even more hideous.

Before we got out of there, Georgie had another tantrum. The checkout girl flat refused to ask Clark, "Who's there?" no matter how many times he said, "Knock-knock." When I grow up and I am a rich, famous artist and embarrassing relatives come knocking on my studio door, I'll be like that checkout girl. I'll ignore the whole bunch and hope they'll go away.

Mama collapsed into her seat while Dad and Jimmy and I loaded all the grocery sacks into the back of the station wagon. "Don't anybody say anything more. I feel like all the air's out of my tires."

"Yeah," said Dad, "everybody just put a sock in it back there."

I didn't say a word, not even when we were almost home and I remembered that we all forgot Mom's sardines *and* her pickles.

"Oh well," she said later on. "We'll pick them up on the way back from my appointment on Friday. Daddy's taking off work to get me to the doctor, and Carmen, you and Jimmy can look after the little ones."

"Will you tell them they have to mind us?"

Harry and Larry made faces at me and stuck out identical tongues. Mom gave all the boys her sternest look and said, "Everyone just be nice."

That was what she always said about the whole world, the Communists over in Russia, Fidel Castro in Cuba, Jews and Arabs in the Middle East, black and white people in America. That went for everybody: just be nice, for crying out loud.

Jimmy, off at the library, taking our books back, got out of babysitting. Not me. I showed Clark and the twins how to make a brontosaurus out of clay.

"Look, you guys, you stick your little fingernail in its face. That makes a smile."

"Make a *Tyrannosaurus rex*!" cried Larry.

"Then he can eat these guys!" Harry growled.

They both roared and bared their teeth as they made their dinosaurs extinct between the palms of their hands and watched cartoons. Georgie's thumb slipped from its mouth socket as he fell asleep on the floor beside all the toys, coloring books, broken crayons, and mashed reptiles.

"Clark, help me pick this stuff up, wouldja?"

"You're not my boss."

He wouldn't quit watching Popeye and Bluto even one second, so I thumped his head—not hard. I'd've tidied up the whole room, but the mailman brought a new magazine with Mrs. Kennedy on the cover. Inside were more pictures of the First Family, plus news that they were going to have another baby too. Maybe it'd have the same birthday as our baby. Maybe they'd invite us to the White House, I thought, as I studied an especially nice picture of Jacqueline Kennedy. Next thing I knew, I was drawing her face on a piece of notebook paper. Anyway, drawing's just daydreaming with a pencil. That's all I was doing when I suddenly got yanked back into my real world.

Where was our blockheaded guardian angel when she was supposed to be protecting Larry when the little dope decided to skip his way downstairs? He didn't bust any bones or even bleed, but did that keep him from howling all the louder when he saw that Mom and Dad were home?

"Was everybody nice?" Mama asked.

No, but I was the only one who got yelled at.

Five

*In which we celebrate Independence Day in Independence.
I learn more about life and death and Richie Scudder.
Robin returns and I'm so happy and then I'm not.*

Already before noon on the Fourth of July, the shimmering air was smoky with firecrackers and Black Cats. It was as hot as the inside of a cow and every bit as humid. Mama decided that she'd stay home with the little kids. She'd put a wet washcloth on her head and take a nap in front of the window fan, something she'd been doing more and more of here lately.

Dad could hardly touch the steering wheel without burning his fingers. He pulled his ball cap low over his eyes and shook his head at Jimmy. "Honey, you gotta wear those durned corduroys today?"

"I'm not too hot, Dad. Honest." If I were a mean person, which I'm *not*, I would say he wore those long britches so no one would see his pudgy white legs.

"Okay, kiddo," Dad said. "To each his own."

"Dad?"

"Yeah, son?"

"Did you know that exactly one hundred years ago today was when they just got done fighting the biggest battle ever in the whole Western Hemisphere? In the Civil War? It was at Gettysburg, Pennsylvania, in *eighteen* sixty-three."

Dad rubbed at his pointy nose. "Wahoo! Is that right?"

Jimmy grinned. "Uh-huh!"

After a load of sweating and band music, we saw the sun bouncing and flashing off the teeny spectacles of a genuine Used-to-Be President of the United States, Harry S. Truman. He said it was great to be in a country where we could say mean things about the fellows in the government and not get thrown in jail, then go fight the whole world to defend our nation if we had to.

"That's right," said Dad under his breath. "I fought for this country and the right to gripe about those knuckleheads in Washington. I swear, President

Kennedy's the only fella in that town who's got any sense."

Between Dad's commenting and the broiling sun over our heads, it was hard to concentrate on Mr. Truman's speech. I thought about Popsicles, or would have if Clark hadn't poked my arm. "Carmie, look at Jimmy. He's getting sick or something."

Sure enough, Jimmy was swaying. I grabbed his hand and said, "Dad!" as a lady behind us exclaimed, "He's fainting!" all in the instant that Jimmy began to fall. Dad caught him and carried him through the crowd. Clark and I passed people squeezing themselves together to make a path for us. A sunburned woman pulled a bottle of orange Nehi out of the cooler at her feet. "Here, hon. Give this to the boy."

"Thanks, ma'am."

President Truman, too far away to know about us, kept on with his speech. Dad set puny-looking Jimmy down in a puddle of shade under a tree by the parking lot. Soon he was drinking the Nehi as Dad fanned him with a newspaper.

"Golly, honey," said Dad, "couldn't you have waited until after the speech to go and faint like that?"

Ker-BLAM!

"A cherry bomb!" someone yelled.

"Some darn kids blew up a trash can over there!"

I still had my hands over my ears when another *boom* came from the same direction: by the cars shimmering in the parking lot. Then there was a series of pop-BANGS, dog barking, and people shouting, "Hey!"

"Some danged fool—!"

"Those tough kids—!"

"They tied firecrackers to that pup!" Dad hollered, and a black, wild-eyed blur whizzed right past us. Zoom-away went Dad and Clark.

"Catch it!" Jimmy shouted, scrambling to his feet and trotting after them.

I just stood next to the tree, both of us rooted to the spot and too smart to be running on a hot day. It was a long time before Clark and Dad came back.

"That dog's probably in Kansas by now," Dad said, wiping his red, sweaty face with the tail of his shirt.

"Where's Jimmy?" I asked, and in the next instant, we looked in the direction of scary sounds: tires squealing, people shouting and screaming.

Dad took a wild look around, then glared at me. "I

thought he was here with you keeping an eye on him!"

"Mister?" Some stranger hollered at Dad, "Is that your kid over there?"

We ran to where four or five sweaty people were bunching around Jimmy. Tears streaked his dirty face, and his corduroys had a rip in them. He'd wrapped his bloody T-shirt around the dog.

"I think she—she's dead!" Jimmy sobbed. "She was running because she was scared, and a car hit her. The person who was driving didn't mean to. I tried to save her, Dad."

"Here now, boy," said Daddy. "Here now. Of course you did. Let me look at her. Maybe she's all right. Maybe she is. You come sit down, son."

I could tell by the look on Dad's face, as he examined the little dog, that it wasn't all right, not at all. Folks clucked their tongues and shook their heads.

Someone said, "That pup's a goner. All's you gotta do is look at it. . . ."

Then we heard a familiar, nasty voice: "Man! I ain't never seen nothin' so funny!"

The people around us turned to look, and they parted so we could see Richie Scudder laughing out loud with his pimple-pussed buddies. "I never seen a dog run so fast: *pop-pop-pop-pop!* Did you get a load of that jelly-bellied kid scrambling to get a hold of that mutt?"

The creeps were too busy cracking themselves up to notice Dad bearing down on them. He grabbed Richie's shirt with one hand and made a fist out of the other. He used the same voice he must have used on tough railroad cops in the bad old days.

"What'd you say?" Dad's arm muscle bulged out his angel harp tattoo. "Did I hear you laughing at my boy?"

"Your boy?" Richie blurted while Dad kept right on, his voice getting louder and louder. "You kids tied gol-durned firecrackers to that pup? You kill a dog and laugh about it?"

"Kill it? We didn't—!" Richie looked over at us, and anybody could tell he didn't know until that minute what'd happened to the dog. Color drained out of his face down into his high-tops. "Look, we was just havin' some fun—"

"Pop him, Dad!" Clark cried. "Sock him in his snot-locker!"

"Take off!" Dad snapped. "Don't let me catch you or your lousy friends messing with no harmless pups or any kid of mine, you got that?"

Richie and his buddies walked away. One of them, when he was a safe distance from Dad, laughed, sort of. Dad snorted air out of his nose. "I should have punched that hoodlum," he growled.

I saw a look on Jimmy's face right then, a determined look that made me see how he would look and be when he became a grown-up man. He ignored Clark telling him how brave he was. He just went off carrying that little dog in the direction of our car.

We were all quiet on the way home. Jimmy got to sit in the front seat. "I'm going to name her Cracker," he said. "You think that's a good name, Dad?"

"Yes, son. A fine name."

Dad buried her in the backyard and helped Jimmy tamp Cracker's scrap board of a grave marker into the ground. We all stood there while Jimmy read, in a steady voice, the Bible verses that began, "The Lord is my shepherd. . . ." I was glad for the dog that she had us to feel bad for her while she was on her way to heaven, but still, her sad funeral made me all the more anxious for nightfall.

At last it came, magic, buggy darkness full of pops, fireflies, and smoke. Georgie got to hold his first sparkler. From across the street, we saw the red spark of old Mr.

Herman's cigar along with its owner coming slowly toward us, to sit with us and watch Larry, Clark, and Harry running across the dark yard trailing smoky light like laughing comets.

Mama and Jimmy pushed the porch swing back and forth with their feet in a slow, comforting rhythm. Was the baby crying or dreaming in there, in Mama's broad, firm middle? Planning what kind of person it was going to be? Was it hearing firecrackers all far away, like corn popping in the kitchen? Did it know what kind of family it had signed up for, or were we all going to be its surprise too? Or did it still have a chance to be born to rich people in Paris? I wished I could talk to Robin about it. She said they'd be back right after the Fourth of July, and anyway, she *had* to be back in time for my birthday next week.

A series of especially loud booms came from up the street. "Oh my goodness!" Mom exclaimed. She smiled down at herself and pressed her hands against her belly. "That woke up the baby."

Old Mr. Herman ran his hand through the tuft of white hair on the top of his head and took his cigar out of his mouth. "I reckon that Scudder boy and his friends must've bought out the inventory at the fireworks tent out on the highway. Now you know," he said, "he wasn't always such a harum-scarum fellow. I can remember when Richard was a good boy, a proper lad, before he lost his mother."

"Well," said Dad, "he's a proper knucklehead now." With that, he walked over to where my mom was a nightcloud in the porch shadows. He bent down to kiss Jimmy's cheek, then Mama's belly and didn't seem to mind at all that smiling Mr. Herman watched him do these things. Daddy handed Mom a sparkler, as if it were a rose, and it lit up her mild, happy face. It was as if, sometimes, my folks were their own family, no matter how many kids came along to mess things up.

"Thirteen years ago, Carmenita, that was you in there," Dad said as he lit another sparkler and handed it to me. "Man, I was never so excited and nervous."

Firecrackers popped, sparked, and danced in the smoky dimness as Mom stroked the top of Jimmy's head. "It's okay. Mama's boy," she murmured. Behind his glasses, Jimmy's eyes were wide and dark.

I was more and more impatient all the next day and the next, waiting for Robin to come back. In the refrigerator was a strawberry cake Mom and I made to pay back Robin's mother. In my sketchbook was a princess I drew to calm myself down. She was on top of her castle by an ocean. Wind blew her gown, her cape, and the silky veil flowing from the tip of her pointed hat. I was going to add a sailing ship for her to see in the distance, but I kept going out on the porch to watch for the Culpeppers' big black car to come around the corner.

"Carmie, stay in or stay out! You're making me a nervous wreck," Mom said, fanning her bright face with a newspaper. "Take these kids up to the playground, why doncha?"

"But it's gonna rain."

"I hope so! Maybe it'll cool things off." She lifted her chin to breathe in little breaths. "Go on now. I need to rest, just a bit. Jimmy, you go too. You need some fresh air."

Jimmy followed me and the little squirts out the door, but he didn't look like he wanted any fresh air nearly as much as he wanted to read his book. The sky over the swings and jungle gym was an angel kingdom full of cloud mountains, all dark and light, looking like a good place for thunder gods and goddesses to have their palaces. I steadied Georgie on his twenty-seventh slide down the sliding board. The other boys were making themselves dizzy on the merry-go-round when we heard a huge thunder-boom. Georgie screamed, half scared, half excited.

"Whoa!" Clark shouted. "Look at the lightning!"

"One-Mississippi, two-Mississippi," Jimmy started counting.

"Come on!" I hollered. "You don't have to know how close it is. We gotta get—" Thunder cracked like a giant whip. Big cold drops plopped on us and polka-dotted the playground. I scooped up Georgie and all us kids ran home through the rain, not noticing that the Culpeppers' big black car was back where it belonged. I didn't even see Robin and her little brother on their front porch until she yelled at me.

"Boy oh boy, Carmen, if anybody ever says you Cathcarts don't know enough to come in out of the rain, I'll tell that person he's full of prunes!"

Over on the Culpeppers' front porch glider, our stories, Robin's and mine, tumbled out and collided into each other.

"Mr. Herman told Jimmy he saw Mrs. Truman up at the store—hey, did you know Richie's got a job there?" I left out Clark embarrassing me with his big mouth and me seeing that cute boy. "Anyway, she was buying a can of pork and beans and . . ."

". . . fireworks in St. Paul and my dad played the piano in a wedding for one of his cousins. I got a new dress for it and . . ."

". . . that poor little dog. You shoulda seen the look on Richie's face when he thought my dad was gonna sock him—hey, the rain stopped!"

"We had to stop the car right by this busy road so Darren could puke from eating seven hot dogs in a row and you shoulda seen my mom . . ."

"Hey, my birthday's next Friday. Did I tell you that?"

"Nope. Mine's October 27th. I wish I'd waited and gotten born on Halloween." Robin shrugged her shoulders. "So are you going to have a party?"

"Not *really.*" My whole insides were buzzing with the good news I'd been saving up and putting off telling, to make it even more exciting. "We're gonna have my cake on Saturday because Dad works Friday, right? He works nights now, but so anyway, listen: my aunt—you're really going to like her—she's going to take off work so she can take us, me and you, to the movies over in Kansas City and go see *Cleopatra*! Won't that be so neat?"

"I'm not sure that would be an appropriate film for Robin."

"Mom!" Robin jumped to her feet; we both did. Had I even noticed Robin's mom in her doorway listening to me?

"No, please!" I said. "My Aunt Bevy's gonna call you and—"

But Mrs. Culpepper had turned her attention to Jimmy, who was carrying a pink-iced cake across the driveway into her yard. "Is that for us? How nice!"

Then she caught sight of her kid over in our yard full of puddles and boys and her smiling mouth scowled. Words began pouring out of it like BBs out of a bucket.

"Darren Albert Culpepper, you're soaking wet! And filthy dirty! You come get cleaned up! Robin, we'll discuss this later. Thank you; what did you say your name was? James? Did you help your mother make this cake? Oh, you did, Carmen? Well, how *very* nice; you and your brother had better run along now. Robin needs to set the table for supper. Darren, leave those *disgusting* sneakers on the porch. We'll see you later. . . ."

Robin signaled me with a quick look at her tree house. Her lips made the word "midnight" as all three Culpeppers went inside and their door clicked shut.

Six

*In which we learn something horrible about Richie the Creep.
Mama and I stay up late on the night of the last day
I'll ever be twelve; she and I get better acquainted.*

"What'd she mean?" Jimmy asked. "Are you and Robin going to the movies?"

"Maybe. Aunt Bevy said she'd take us for my birthday."

"I wanna go."

"I don't think so."

Wasn't it bad enough that Old Yeller might not let Robin go with me and Aunt Bevy? Did I want to share my birthday with a little brother? Not exactly.

Jimmy stomped up the steps behind me and let the screen door slam. "Robin's my friend too!"

82

"Hush up!" Dad said. He jerked his thumb at Mom sleeping on the couch. "Jimmy, you clear the junk off the table and Carmen can peel some taters while I open up some cans and rustle up supper. Your mama's not feelin' good."

Later, when I was up high enough to look over the edge of the boards in the tree, an eerie moon face floating in the branches spoke to me: "It is eight minutes past midnight." Then Robin switched off the flashlight under her chin and helped me up into her office.

"You are so weird," I panted. "Did Aunt Bevy call your mom? I called and asked her to. Did your mom say you could go?"

"Your aunt called and Mom said she and Dad would think about it."

"Well, anyway, I'm glad you're here and not in Minnesota."

There didn't seem like much else to say. We lay on our backs, feet propped in the branches, eating our strawberry cake. Our street was dark and quiet until—

"What was that?" I whispered. It sounded like a creaky screen door.

"I didn't hear anything." But she couldn't help hearing what came next: an angry rumble of voices from the Scudder house. Yelling, too far away to hear all the words, close enough to hear the meanness.

"It's Richie's dad," Robin said under her breath.

"Huh? You think we ought to go see what's happening?"

"I *know* what's happening. Ever since Mrs. Scudder died, he gets real noisy sometimes."

"When did she?"

"Two or three years ago. Richie was in ninth grade, I think."

We heard a twig snap, then footsteps down below! Robin grabbed her flashlight, but she didn't need it. The street lamp and a couple of porch lights were enough for us to see who it was.

"Hey, Jimmy! Stop!" We shouted as loud as we could and still be whispering, but he just kept walking in the direction of Richie Scudder's house.

Boy, I'd never gone down that stupid rope ladder so fast! Robin and I hurried over to Mr. Scudder's pickup truck, where Jimmy stood in the blackest shadows, light glinting off his glasses. We jumped at the sound of a man's voice, ugly and angry.

"I'm glad your mother's not around to see what a bum you turned out to be!"

"This is dangerous," I hissed, but still, we kept inching through the dark, like trouble was a magnet pulling on us.

"Listen, old man, I got a job," we heard Richie say.

"Don't you sass me, boy!" Mr. Scudder thundered. I felt more than saw Jimmy's shoulders cringe when we heard a thump and hitting sounds.

"Stop it, man, you're hurtin' me!"

"You're gol-durn right I'm hurtin' ya, you lazy, worthless—"

"Come on," I hissed, "let's go *now*. We shouldn't be here."

"His dad is so mean," Jimmy whispered when we got to our yard.

"Still . . . Richie was rotten to do what he did to Cracker. She was just a poor little dog."

"Yeah, well, maybe his horrible dad is why Richie's so creepy," said Robin.

The night was quiet again, like Richie's crummy dad had settled down for the night. I wished ours had when he caught Jimmy and me sneaking in.

"Don't *even* tell me what you're doing up at this

hour," said Dad. "I don't want to know. It's too danged late."

"Why were *you* out there, *James?*" I asked when it was just us. "You were spying on Robin and me, weren't you?"

You wouldn't think a person could yawn and push his slippy glasses up and still look sly, but Jimmy could. "I just wanted to see if Robin can go to the movies with us," he said.

Almost all of the night before I turned thirteen, I couldn't sleep. Maybe if I weren't so excited about Robin's mom giving in and saying she could go to the movies, I could've slept, if it weren't so hot and sticky. My eyes kept opening and seeing pale rectangles. All around me, thumbtacked to the walls and ceiling, were all of my lady drawings. They were so beautiful. It was nice, knowing they were there, and fun, imagining them talking among themselves when I was away. Their gowns fluttered in the warm breeze from the window fan, which couldn't seem to cool one single inch of my bed. My pillow felt like a hot water bottle and besides, I heard voices downstairs.

Avoiding the creaky places on the steps, I tiptoed

down and past my parents' empty bedroom and the boys' room, and on down until I could tell where the voices were coming from: the television. It'd been turned so it could shine out of the open front window. Beyond it was the slightly cooler outdoors, the porch swing, and Mom, watching the late movie.

I slipped out of the front door as quietly as I could, but the squeaky spring on the screen door let her know I was there. Mom patted the swing beside her and, with a glance at her belly, whispered, "This child can't sleep either." She breathed in a couple of shallow sips of air. "It's probably as hot and humid in there as it is out here, poor thing. Well, we can watch the movie together and tell Daddy hello when he comes home from work." I returned Mom's smile in the dark.

"He'll like that," I whispered. We almost never got to be just us two, Mama and me. The chains squeaked and protested as I sat down next to her.

"Goodness," Mama said, stroking my hair, "look how long this has gotten. We'll want to trim those bangs before Bevy comes tomorrow. Maybe you'll let me French braid it like I did when you were little."

Her hand felt nice, but I had my private doubts about bang trimming and braids. Moms can do some

87

weird damage when they start messing with your hair.

"It's your Birthday Eve!" she went on. "There should be a custom for that, don't you think? Like hanging up a stocking?"

"We could leave cookies and milk for the birthday fairy."

Mama chuckled.

"Or," I suggested hopefully, "I could open my presents after midnight."

"In the morning," she told me, "like a proper birthday. And I saved an extra present for Saturday, when we have your cake and candles."

"What is it?"

"A surprise, that's what. Shush, now. You'll want to hear this movie. It's *National Velvet*."

We'd been whispering like I imagined girls did when they stayed all night at their friends' houses. Moths and june bugs were fluttering, hurling themselves at the window screen, crazy to get at the glowing pictures of a dark-haired girl ("That's Elizabeth Taylor," said Mama) and a running horse.

The night was dark and sweet smelling, like the inside of a lady's black purse. A cool breeze ruffled through the trees. When the movie gave way to a commercial, Mama began whispering again.

"I'm glad they're showing this. My mom—your grandma—took Bev and me to see *National Velvet* when I wasn't much older than you are now. It was my favorite." According to Mom, this old movie was about more than Velvet Brown and Pi, her horse, and their winning a big race. "It's about Velvet's mother there, and how she and her daughter shared their dreams. They both had high hopes."

"What were your high hopes?" I asked.

"Well . . ."

"Did you have a dream?"

"Oh." Mama paused. "Well you know, your father and I—when he got home from the war and we got married . . . Well, we wanted you children. I guess you could say that was our dream, a nice big family—"

It sounded like a nightmare to me. "Why?" I interrupted.

Even in the darkness, I could see she looked surprised. "Babies are a gift from God!" she said, a lot more firmly than she usually talked.

"Not much of a present" was the thought that popped out of the bratty part of my brain. Another crybaby thought tumbled right out after it: each new kid only

89

pushed her farther away from me, from the time I was her only one.

"Why did we have to have such a big family? I mean, we could have just been Jimmy for Daddy. And—" I was ashamed to say the babyish rest of it: and me for her. I had *some* pride.

Mama pressed her cool hand to the side of my face. "Oh Carmen," she said, ignoring the movie that had started again. "How can I tell you how it was for your dad and me? The war and the Depression years before that, when we were kids, they'd been so hard. So when I first found out that I was . . ." Mama's hand rose to fiddle with her hair. "When I was going to have a baby, we were so happy, but then something happened and—" Her voice faltered. "And, well, I lost the baby."

"Lost it?" My own voice was small. Of course I knew she hadn't misplaced the baby or left it somewhere. I couldn't stand to think of her being sick or in trouble.

"It was a medical thing," she went on. "Things— pregnancies, I mean—sometimes go wrong. We were both so sad, and then, when it happened again—"

"Again? That happened to you two times? That there wasn't going to be a baby after all?" I squeezed her rough hand.

"It was almost worse for your poor dad," said Mama. She looked out into the night, as if she could see him out there, with his head in his hands out in some long-ago yard. "Then you came along." She smiled. "You were so cuddly and happy. You were a dream come true."

Her words made my throat tight and tears sting my nose. Okay, I was pretty desperate for her to say something mushy like that.

"And even on your worst day, you still are." She put her arms around me and hugged me to her big softness. Mama smelled like face powder, baby powder, and graham crackers. "This baby will be a dream come true, too, Carmie. You'll see."

Dad's headlights swooped around the corner as the movie ended and, back inside the house, our clock chimed midnight. Mama hugged me even tighter and told me, "Happy birthday."

Seven

In which I become thirteen, I imagine Egypt,
I learn about America and the real world.

I sat between Robin and Aunt Bevy in an old Kansas City movie palace, our faces turned up to the big screen, watching the magnificently eye-shadowed Queen of the Nile. Only a few hours earlier, I'd been sitting beside Mama, watching this same actress, Elizabeth Taylor, pretending to be (National) Velvet Brown, back when she was my age and probably not allowed to wear all that makeup.

I covered my third yawn with my hand. "Don't you like the movie?" Aunt Bevy whispered into my ear,

"You're not bored are you?"

"No! I love it! I stayed up too late last night, that's all."

Her lips twitched. She pointed at the person on her other side. Jimmy, who'd won a hard campaign to come with us, was sound asleep.

Cleopatra was the best grown-up movie I'd ever seen, and we got to see it on the best day I'd ever lived, so far. Jimmy and I hardly ever got to go to the movies, much less have grilled cheese sandwiches in a city restaurant with tablecloths and waiters. Robin and I saw a man wink at my aunt, so glamorous in her orange dress and shocking pink shoes to match her purse. My purse didn't match anything, but it was stuffed with presents: my own personal yo-yo and a tube of pale lipstick, plus a compact with powder puff. Around my neck was Jimmy's macaroni necklace. At home, up in my room, was Clark's yellow clay stegosaurus, three specially-scribbled, torn-out coloring book pages from the twins and Georgie and, from the folks, a blue plastic transistor radio complete with dangly earplug.

Back in the hot, glittery outdoors, I still had tears in my eyes from how Cleopatra's story ended.

Robin flung both her arms out wide. "Absolutely excellent!"

"I'll say!" said Jimmy, blinking and squinting his eyes.

Aunt Bevy winked at me from behind her bejeweled sunglasses.

"But it was too sad at the end," Robin went on. "Didn't you think so, Miss Gillespie?"

Aunt Bevy nodded her beehive hairdo. "That was the best part," she said, blowing her nose and flicking a tear from her eye with a pink-polished fingertip. All the way to where her little car was parked, we talked about the movie. Aunt Bevy's pink high heels click-click-clicked on the bright, hard sidewalk.

"At least poor Cleopatra died glamorously," I said, "in her very own palace, with a serpent." My private plan was to draw the beautiful dying queen as soon as I got home to my paper and pencils.

"How about if she just told both of those Roman guys to go soak their heads in a bucket," said Robin. "Then she could rule Egypt all by herself."

"There's a thought!" Aunt Bevy exclaimed. "That's what I'd've done."

Did the people in ancient Egypt and Rome know

they were ancient or did they think they were modern? Will people in the far-off future think that 1963 is ancient, I wondered? I fingered my French-braided hair, all sleek and knobby, thanks to Mom.

Aunt Bevy drove us through shadowy canyons of buildings, tapping her fingers on her steering wheel, keeping time with "Sugar Shack" on the radio. She pointed out the department store where she worked. "Shame we don't have time for you kids to meet everybody."

We wrinkled our noses at the smells of buses, cars' tailpipes, and street pavement gone spongy in the heat. As we waited at a red light, a group of black people crossed the street in front of us. My eyes caught on the men's thin shirts and narrow-brimmed straw hats, the women's hats and sleeveless summer dresses. Aunt Bevy rested her head on her hand. "I wonder how they're all feeling about what's going on these days in this country," she said, more to herself than to us.

"My dad talks a lot about how people get treated," said Robin, "just for trying to vote, or go to school, or ride buses like everybody else. It's not fair."

"They talked about those things on the news," Jimmy added, "and you know what Mama said?"

I nodded. "I bet she wished everyone would just be nice."

"It's a good idea," Aunt Bevy said. She flicked her lipsticky cigarette butt out the window. "Whew!" she said, sighing, and wasn't it hot?

At our house Harry and Larry rocketed out the screen door like snakes out of a can. Darren Culpepper and Clark sat on the roof of the porch, dangling and kicking their feet. "Daddy's gone to work," Clark called out. "He said to tell you happy birthday, Buddy!"

"You and Darren get away from that edge, you idiots," I yelled, "before you fall off of there!"

"Look, Carmie, my tooth fell out!" Harry hollered, pointing at the hole in his grin as he climbed up on the curved front of Aunt Bevy's car. "Georgie's been a brat."

"But not us," said Larry. "Except Harry broke the light in the front room after Mom told him not to throw his ball in the house."

"Did not!"

Robin, Jimmy, and I climbed out of the car. Aunt Bevy hollered up at Clark, "Say there, how's your mama?"

"She's okay! She's in the kitchen cooking tomatoes and putting 'em in jars!"

"In this heat?" Aunt Bevy's high heels went clicking up our walk. At the sight of totally naked Georgie running out of the house, Robin and I made faces at each other. Aunt Bevy picked him up as she flounced into the house, letting the screen door slap shut behind her.

"Thanks for the movie, Miss Gillespie!" Robin called out. "Happy birthday, Carmen! See ya later!"

Her dad, who was over locking up their front door, turned and said, "Perfect timing! We were waiting for you. I can tell you had a good time." Mrs. Culpepper was hurrying to her side of the big, black car, cradling a covered dish in her right arm and checking her watch on the left.

"Darren!" Mr. Culpepper called. "Get your ridiculous little self down *off* that roof and come get in the car. We're due over to Uncle Lloyd and Aunt Margie's." After plenty of "So long, happy birthday"s and slamming car doors, they were gone.

When I went inside, Aunt Bevy was scolding Mama. "Dee-dee, you sit yourself down, right now, over here. You look like you're about to melt. What are you thinking of—canning tomatoes when the whole outdoors is an oven and you're about to pop! Are you out of your mind?"

97

Aunt Bevy stood tiptoe in her high heels so she could adjust the clothespins on our bedsheet curtains. She picked her way through our regular, everyday clutter of toys and coloring books to aim the window fan at her sister. It blew Mama's damp hair in floaty curls around her face. Aunt Bevy rescued the knocked-down straw castle, all tangled around a red rubber ball and baby tricycle handlebars, and hung it on the freshly busted *Sputnik* chandelier.

"These boys've been pretty wild all day," said Mama. "I wanted to get the canning done up before the baby comes. Did you have a good time? Everybody behave themselves?"

"Yes, we did have a good time and everybody had nice manners, but as for you! Canning! In your condition! As if there weren't plenty of tomatoes in tin cans up at the store!"

Boy, that's just what I was thinking! The mild look on Mama's flushed face showed perfectly well that she knew Aunt Bevy wasn't really mad at her. She petted Harry's and Larry's heads as they pressed their ears against her light green dress and knocked their little knuckles on her hard belly. "Come out, baby," they called in soft voices.

"Whew!" said Aunt Bevy. "That baby might want to stay inside of you, Dee, where it's cooler. Might as well be in the jungles of Borneo as Missouri in July!" She leaned down and kissed Mama on the forehead.

"I'll call you later, sweet thang. Got me a date tonight. You need any help 'round here before I take off? Anything from the store?" She slapped her forehead with her hand. "Oh for crying out loud, it's a good thing my head's screwed on! Carmie, run out and get me that sack under the front seat."

Aunt Bevy dug around in it and pulled out a jar of sweet pickles and a tin of sardines. "Here you go, Dee-dee. I hope these aren't too cooked, being in my car all day. I know how you like 'em when you got a baby goin'."

"Bless your heart, Bevy." Mama smiled up at her. "I'll have 'em for dessert tonight."

Clark and Larry crossed their eyes and pretended to puke.

Aunt Bevy bent down and put her cheek against Mama's hair. "Are you sure I can't do anything for you?"

"No, no," Mama said. "You go on. Carmen can help me with supper and anything else. Call me tomorrow and tell me about your date."

* * *

Up in my room, I yanked off the dress I wore into the city. I pulled on cutoffs and one of Dad's shirts, got my drawing pad and pencils, and hurried back downstairs to grab the C book from the encyclopedia. I had to look up "Cleopatra."

Jimmy lifted his own book up and out of the way so I could plop down, fling my legs across onto his lap, and prop my feet on the arm of the couch. My fingers absolutely itched to draw the queen of Egypt—her snaky crown, her beaded necklace, her white gown. Would I show her on her barge on the River Nile? Too hard to draw all those rowing guys. Smooching the Roman emperor? Too sappy. Mama slowly rose from her chair as I pictured Cleopatra's eyes, like black fishes with jewels. I'd only have to draw one of 'em if I drew a side view. And a sideways nose was easier to draw, I was thinking, as Mama patted one of my bare feet. The floorboards creaked as she walked past me, putting her hand on my head. "Say there, Birthday Girl, why don't you clear off the table for me, here in a little bit?"

"Okay."

She ruffled Jimmy's hair with her fingers. Clark and Harry took turns clicking the channel dial, making images flit and sputter across the television. Carefully Mama walked off toward the kitchen, around Georgie and Larry's block tower, the hem of her light green dress skimming the top of Georgie's head.

Just as Jimmy turned his page, just as I was drawing a pyramid behind the queen of Egypt, we all jumped at the sounds of a gasp and breaking glass, and the real world came crashing in on us.

The whole kitchen was red.

Mama's back was bowed, and she was holding tight to her stomach. Her other hand gripped the edge of the table. Between the freckles, the skin of her knuckles was white. Tomatoes and smashed glitters of glass were swimming in tomatoey water and a redder, darker wet—everywhere, soaking into boxes, pooling around pots set to soak. Blood!

Mama turned her streaming face to me. She grabbed my hand hard and gasped out, "The baby. Carmie, it's the baby."

"What do I do? What do I do!" I was almost screaming; then Mama sagged against me. I grabbed a chair and sat so my lap could help hold her and keep her from falling on the awful floor. My mind snapped down to business, ice-cube cold. I shouted at the wild-eyed, blubbering boys, "Get out of here! Get away! There's glass all over the place! You don't have your shoes on! Out! Get OUT of here! Clark, don't just stand there. Bring me towels! HURRY!"

Harry shouted at me, "Carmie! What's the matter? What's wrong with her?"

"Mommy!" Bawling Georgie tried to claw his way through Larry's legs to get into the kitchen. Jimmy's shocked face appeared in the doorway, then vanished.

"She's bleeding!" Larry shrieked.

"Shut UP!" I yelled. "Larry, take Georgie in the other room! Jimmy!" The front door slammed as Clark burst into the kitchen with a bundle of towels.

"He ran outside. Did Mama cut herself?"

"*Outside?* Clark, can you get the telephone cord to stretch into here? I gotta call the doctor or Daddy to come home!"

"Maybe you better ought to call an ambulance!"

"Yeah, okay, bring me the phone book—hurry, Clark! Then go—oh, take the little ones upstairs and try to settle 'em down." Dumb to think that anybody would be calm.

I cradled Mama's head in my lap. My shaking fingers were scrambling for the right number to call when an urgent-sounding voice demanded, "Where is she?"

"In the kitchen," said Jimmy. Hard-heeled feet came stomping through the house and Richie Scudder burst into our kitchen. Maybe if I suddenly saw Elvis Presley I would've been more shocked, but I don't think so.

Somehow, in the next crowded, horrible, five-minute-long eternity, Richie and Jimmy and I got Mama into the backseat of his old Cadillac. "We're gettin' you to the hospital," said Richie, real gentle. "You'll be okay, ma'am."

"Okay," she whispered. Mama's eyes opened wide then squinched tight shut, and she pressed her lips together as a hard hurt took her. Then she tried to smile at me. "Be a big girl and look after the little ones. I'm counting on you, Carmie."

Jimmy hopped in, and they roared away with Mama.

"Mom!" Clark shouted. "Good-bye, Mom!"

I ran into the street to catch Georgie. "Mommy!" he screamed. "Come back! Mommy! Don't!" he cried, chasing after Richie's car. I grabbed him, and he struggled in my arms out in the middle of the street until the car disappeared around the corner. "Don't go away!" he wailed. "Mommy!"

Clark turned to me, wiping his eyes with the backs of his hands. "I'll go call Daddy at the factory, okay?"

My lips made the word "okay," but no sound came out of them. I felt the neighbors' stares. Mr. Herman, his milkweed hair all white and wild, was standing on his porch steps. I swallowed hard and called to him and the Monroe ladies out in their zinnia beds. "We're okay," I lied. "Mom's having the baby."

Miss Effie cupped her gloved hands around her mouth. "Mercy!"

"You be sure and let us know what kind she has," said Miss Lillian, "girl or boy!"

I waved and nodded my head at the ladies. Mr. Herman looked both ways, then set off across the street to us as I said to the boys, real soft, "We don't be crying in front of all the neighbors, okay?" As if crying weren't the most sensible thing anyone could do in such a moment. I lied to them, too: "It'll be all right."

Georgie buried his face in my neck, and Larry sniffled. With the back of his hand he dashed away his tears, like he was too big to be crying in front of Mr. Herman. Harry, with his thumb in his mouth, wasn't quite so proud.

"Now there," said Mr. Herman, crinkling his eyes at me. "I wasn't spying and I don't like to barge in on you just when you've got your hands full." He shifted his cane to his other knobby hand so he could pat Larry's shoulder.

"I just happened to see the way your little brother— now, James didn't come to me, he knew *I* didn't have no car no more!—and that wild Scudder boy went tearing off with your mom and the way them little fellers were carrying on. I could see that you were having a bad day. You say the baby's comin'?"

"I think so." I gulped. "Thank you for . . . you're really, really nice to come check on us, but . . ."

I thought Mr. Herman was searching his pockets for peppermints, but instead he dug out a bent calling card and held it out to me. "This here's got my phone number. Now you call if you need any little thing. You fellas help your big sister, okay?"

"Okay, Mr. Herman, we will," said Larry, in a way that made me think I wasn't the only one who was thinking, "*Just go away* and quit being so blasted nice before I start bawling in front of you." We were in terrible trouble and I couldn't even stand to think how much help we needed. I herded the boys into the house and leaned my back against the closed front door.

"I told a guy at Dad's work to tell him about Mom," said Clark. "Do you think he's at the hospital now?"

"Probably. He'll call us any minute now, I bet, to tell us about Mom and the new baby." I put an arm around Clark's bony shoulders. "You wanna help me . . . uhm . . . let's clean up the kitchen a little bit?"

Clark and I attacked the splintery mess; then I stuck Band-Aids over the places we'd cut ourselves. Beside the sink were Mama's presents from Aunt Bevy. Dumb how a pickle jar and a stupid tin of sardines made me feel even more terrible. I stuck them in a cupboard and went down to the cellar. I plunged the stained towels into the washtub, then pulled my shirt over my head and shoved it in too. Blood moved like red smoke, like mermaids' hair in the water. I shivered and rubbed at the goose bumps on my arms. Why hadn't Jimmy or Dad or anybody called from the hospital?

The soft thumps and voices of the television and the boys sifted down through the ceiling beams. From Mama's rainy day clothesline, laundry hung like a row of ghosts in the gloom. I yanked off a shirt and put it on, then, like Mama probably used to do, I stood listening to the sounds of everyone's voices and footsteps up above the dangly wires and spiderwebby house beams. It was comfortable, in a strange sort of way, to hear everybody from this little distance. Down here, away from them all, you could appreciate the *idea* of our family. It felt like a glimpse of the mom I hadn't known, like I understood her better, somehow.

What was happening to her? What were they doing to her?

I headed back up the cellar steps, away from the rush of feelings that came with my memory of Mama's face and what she'd said to me.

All of the boys were scattered about the front room, each with cereal bowls full of ice cream. "Ice cream always makes things better," Clark said meekly. I smoothed his hair. "Good idea, kid."

"Mom got it to go with your birthday cake," said Harry. An almost empty ice-cream box was leaking all over the table. I popped a spoonful of it in my mouth and put the box in the freezer. The phone rang.

Clark won the scramble of "I'll get it"s. "Daddy? . . . Okay, okay, here she is."

He scowled. "He just wants to talk to you."

I grabbed the phone away from him. "Is Mom okay?"

"Carmen?" Dad said. "Is that you?" I could hear people talking in a busy background. "Well, we got us a baby—"

"How's Mama?" My question collided with Dad's news. I blew out a big breath and told the boys, "Mama had a girl!"

"Yuck!" Larry shouted, wrinkling his nose in mock disgust at Harry, who clapped his hands. Clark stood staring at me, worry frozen on his face while the littler ones jumped up and down and tugged on my clothes. "When's Mommy coming home? Lemme talk to her! Lemme talk!"

"Be quiet, you guys!" I stuck a finger in my ear so I could hear Dad say, "Carmie? Are you all okay?"

"Yeah, we're fine, but you didn't tell me how's Mama? Are Richie and Jimmy there?"

"They're right here. That Scudder boy's gonna bring Jimmy home in a little bit, but listen, honey, I gotta go. Your mama's not—she's not doin' so good. Now the baby's fine; she's just perfect, but . . ." I heard Daddy clear his throat.

"What?"

"Now Carmie, I got hold of Beverly, and she said she'd stay there with you all tonight. The baby hadn't showed up yet, so Bevy doesn't know. You go on and tell her and . . . oh, I don't know." I gripped the phone tighter while Daddy paused. "It, uhm . . . it may be late before I can get home."

My whole insides felt like a cave full of bats. My face must've been pretty scared looking because even Georgie piped down. "Daddy? Don't go!" I pleaded. "What's the matter?"

"I gotta go, honey. They're callin' me. Say your prayers."

He clicked off and I hung up.

If things were normal around our house, if I wasn't needing to be here with the boys, I'd have run up to my room. Of course, if things *were* normal, I wouldn't be standing by the phone trying not to cry in front of them, because Mama would be here. But she wasn't, and things were rotten.

It wasn't much later when Clark ran to the window. "Aunt Bevy's here!" The boys followed her in the door. Her makeup was smudged and her beehive hairdo had come loose since she'd taken us to the movies way back a million years ago.

"I just got in the door when your dad phoned," she said, sounding out of breath. "I didn't even call the fella I was supposed to go out with tonight. I speeded all the way back over here, and I think I ran a red light! Carmen, what on Earth—? Your mom was fine when I left. What happened? Has she had the baby?"

Telling Aunt Bevy made me see everything all over again in my mind. "It was right after you left. In the kitchen—Mom was bleeding. She was hurting real bad." I choked out the words and couldn't stop a tear from rolling down my cheek. "It was because of the baby."

Aunt Bevy pulled me to her in a hard squeeze.

"It's a girl," said Clark. "That's what Dad said."

I heard Aunt Bevy say, "Oh my!" and my own thick voice: "He said to say our prayers."

I pulled away from her, wiping my eyes, but Aunt Bevy kept tight hold of my hand. She pursed her lips and looked at all of us Cathcarts, then, for a little bit, down at her pointy-toed shoes. She stepped out of one high heel, then out of the other, pushed a toy truck aside with her stockinged foot, and knelt down on her knees on our front room floor. With a twirl of her hand, she motioned for us to kneel down beside her.

"Fold your hands," I told the boys, "and close your eyes."

Aunt Bevy's hoarse voice began, "Our Father, who art in Heaven . . ."

It was late. The ten-o'clock news had started and Robin's family had come back home from visiting their relatives. Lights were on over there. It seemed strange that Robin was right next door and didn't know yet that anything was wrong. Aunt Bevy and I had finally gotten Georgie and the twins in bed. A car stopped out front.

Two doors slammed. I saw Jimmy and Richie get out and come up the walk, their heads bowed-down tired. They climbed the steps into the moth flutter around the porch light. It glowed on Jimmy's glasses, then haloed Richie's summer crew cut. His eyes darted around at all of us as he followed Jimmy into the room. My eyes kept going to their blood-stained T-shirts. Without a quiver, without even a hi, Jimmy looked at me hard and said, "I think Mama's going to die."

"What?" I looked over at Richie, then back to Jimmy, who wouldn't answer me, just headed up the stairs.

"What?" I pulled at his shirt. "Did the doctors—? Did Dad tell you that?" I sputtered, grabbing his arm. "Did you hear the nurses say something?"

He only frowned and scrunched his head down and away from me, like I was hitting him. "I don't know! I just think she is! Leave me alone!" He yanked his arm away and trudged up the stairs.

Aunt Bevy had been sitting on the couch with sleeping Clark using her lap for a pillow. Now she struggled out from under him to follow after Jimmy.

Richie glanced at me from under his eyebrows as he stalked out of the house. I ran to catch the screen door before it slammed. "What happened?" I called after him.

He stopped in the middle of our cracked walk and rubbed the back of his neck before he turned around. "They all seemed kind of worried and runnin' around, I guess," he said. "Look, I ain't no doctor, kid."

Richie seemed different, kind of older, somehow, than before. Maybe it was because now I knew more about him. Plus he'd helped Mama. I followed him as he walked to his car. "Thank you for all—" I leaned down so I could look at him through the passenger window. "Thank you for all you did."

He started up the engine and turned on the head-lights before he spoke, without ever once looking me in the eye. "Yeah, well, I was just glad the kid came and got me. Must not've been anyone else around with a car."

"He must've thought you could help." I rested my hand on the car door. I started to say, "Imagine that," but it'd sound too dumb.

"Anyway," he muttered, "maybe it made up, kind of, for that trouble with the dog and all. . . ." He gave a little snort. "Oh yeah, your kid brother said it was your birthday." Real quick, he directed his eyes at mine, then back to the lit-up dashboard. "Some day, huh?" His hand reached itself toward mine, like people do some-times: pat your hand, comforting-like. Just in time he snatched his hand away and said, "Look, I hope your mom's okay." Then he jammed his car into gear, and I jumped back. Richie Scudder roared up the black street away from our house and screeched around the corner, and the sound of his engine faded into the night.

I sat out on the front steps, leaning against the porch post. I looked up and down the quiet street at the porch lights and gleams of light shining through whirring window fans. Mr. Herman's bungalow was dark. So was the house where the Monroe ladies lived. The treetops were blowing black in the cool night breeze, like God was breathing down, like guardian angels were fluttering their wings.

"Things sometimes go wrong," Mama had said. Please, please, I prayed. A sharp smell of cigarette smoke interrupted my memory and my hoping. Aunt Bevy had turned off the porch light and come outside.

"Did you call over to the hospital?"

"Just now." She paused. "The nurse said that your father's on the way home."

"What else did she say?"

I couldn't see her face. She was just a construction paper silhouette against the front room window. The spark at the end of her cigarette flowered orange as she inhaled more smoke. "What did she say?" I asked her again, louder this time, and I held my breath.

My face felt cold.

Aunt Bevy wiped at her eye with the heel of her hand, like Georgie does when he needs a nap. She sniffed, and I heard a soft sob come from her throat.

Another sound made me turn to see Jimmy at his bedroom window. Headlights came around our corner. Our old Rambler shot up the driveway, then the engine fell into a deep, humming sort of silence.

You wanted to hold on to such a quiet.

Eight

*In which some of us Cathcarts cry in front
of the neighbors after all. They bring us food,
and the Culpeppers come inside our house.*

*Don't even get out of the car, Daddy. Just sit in there like you're
doing and don't even say what you're going to say.*

But the car door swung open. Daddy climbed out
and leaned his back against the side of the old station
wagon and rubbed the angel harp on his arm. My tough-
guy, sort of jolly dad had been replaced by the saddest
man in the world. He lifted up his head to Aunt Bevy
and me. "The doctors were in there forever trying
everything. . . ."

I went over and put my arms around him, and he
crushed me into his warm, sweaty chest. "Your mama's

116

gone. She's—really gone, and what the hell am I ever gonna do without her?" His voice smashed into sobs.

I'd never seen my dad cry. Or Aunt Bevy. She moaned long and sorrowful as her legs gave way. She sank down onto the grass and cried—no, she wailed.

"Dee! Oh Dee!"

One by one thoughts came into my mind, like stones plunking into water, like actors walking out on an empty black stage carrying cards: YOUR MOTHER IS GONE. NOT COMING BACK. Never to see her? Not hear her voice ever again? "Babies are a gift," she said. Was this some kind of a God joke? Like this baby was some cosmic birthday present? Like God was saying, "Okay, Carmen, I'll take your mother and here, you can have a baby sister. Don't ask me why 'cause I won't tell you." And if every kid had pushed Mama farther away from me, this last baby had pushed her clear out to heaven, to where none of us could follow till only God knew when.

If only there hadn't *been* a stupid baby in the first place! I pulled away from Dad and went to sit on the front porch steps. I pressed my face into the private nest my arms made when I hugged them around my knees. I tried to shut out Aunt Bevy's loud crying, the

117

sounds of doors, boys shouting, running footsteps. Someone's hand was petting my hair, soft arms trying to hug me. Robin saying, "You're kidding!" and "What?" and "NO!" and "Carmen, don't cry."

I wasn't. Not like Clark, bawling somewhere inside the dark house.

"Leave me alone." I struggled to my feet and ran into the house, not letting myself even look at Robin. I made my way upstairs, keeping my face turned away from my folks' room, trying not to hear Jimmy sobbing on the other side of my bedroom wall.

Me, I just felt too surprised and mad to cry. I lay on my bed, in the dark, my fingers wrapped around the tip of the braid Mama had made for me this morning.

When the sun was barely up Saturday morning, everybody else was asleep. The air was so cool, the light was so soft, a person could almost believe that she dreamed last night. But Mama wasn't in the basement or anywhere, and I missed her so bad. I was wishing so much that she'd come out on the porch and say, "Good morning. You're up early."

I jumped when I heard the screen door open. Daddy came to sit close beside me on the porch steps, and we tried to smile at each other. He took a sip from his coffee cup. "I'd've brought you a bowl of cornflakes or something if I'd known you were out here, honey. You okay?"

"No."

One corner of his mouth turned up. "Me either." His face was stubbly, and his eyes looked like he'd been crying instead of sleeping, but he had a clean blue shirt on and his red hair looked wet and combed.

"Are you going somewhere?"

"I gotta go sign some papers at the hospital. And see the baby."

"Will you bring her home?"

"No, she's had a hard time too. The nurses said it'd be Tuesday or Wednesday, most likely, but I could bring you kids to see her before then."

I was scared. Our old crib was in a corner of Mom and Dad's room. Mama had a big box full of baby things somewhere, but were we ready? "Dad, will we know how to take care of her?"

He bowed his head and seemed to cave in on himself. A muscle moved in his jaw.

I leaned my shoulder up against his. "I guess we'll figure it out, huh?"

He nodded his head and, for a long while, seemed to be thinking how to say something. When he did, he surprised me. "Carmie, they're gonna wanna name for the baby. You got any ideas?"

All kinds of feelings came into me along with the best name this baby could have. I told Dad and told him why it was so perfect. He rested his head on the top of mine. "That's a beautiful name. It's as good as Carmen Louise. Your mom'd think so too, I bet."

Later that morning, when Dad got back from visiting the baby, our neighbors started visiting us. A hundred years from now when I'm a ghost or an angel with all of the other dead people, I bet I'll still remember everybody crying and being nice to us.

Mr. Herman brought a store-bought lemon pie. "Oh, Mr. Cathcart," he said, taking hold of Dad's hand in both of his. "I couldn't be more sorry. I lost my bride of forty years, and I still miss her. . . ."

Was Mama somewhere watching the tidy Culpeppers come inside our messy house after all?

Robin's mom brought a casserole. Tuna noodle. And there wasn't any meanness in her pale eyes. Plenty of curiosity, though, as she and Mr. Culpepper took in our jumble of books, toys, and bewildered boys everywhere.

Our too-sad-to-shave, sleepwalker-zombie dad. Tight-faced me heading for the stairs after too much looking at Robin's family looking at all of us. Robin followed me up a couple of steps. "Carmen?"

She was all pale except for red splotches on her cheeks. "Can I come up with you?" When I was all set to be by myself before I started bawling in front of everybody? To see my crummy room?

Oh, so what. Who cared. "Sure," I said. "If you want to."

Her footsteps followed mine up, up, up.

I leaned against the door to my room and folded my arms as her blue eyes swept across my rumpled sheets, my clothes scattered and draped over stacks of books, and the magazines I'd been copying pictures out of. She smiled, kind of, at my old Tiny Tears doll sitting next to Clark's stegosaurus on top of the green book-case scribbled over with lipstick, thanks to baby Harry. I saw her notice my curtainless window; then Robin put her fingertips to her parted lips and looked kind of amazed at all of my pictures on the walls. She leaned forward to study each one, tilting her head this way and that, her black ponytail swishing down her back. "Did you draw all of these?"

"Yeah."

She looked hard at my picture of Venus. I'd copied her out of the Botticelli book. It wasn't very good. The goddess's face was sort of gray where I had to do a lot of erasing.

"Wow, Carmen, these are so neat."

Did she really think so? She could just be feeling sorry for me and cheering me up, but she kept looking at my pictures. Then Robin plopped down on my bed. "I didn't know you were such a good artist."

Her saying that and being so nice made my throat tight. She frowned down at her hands in her lap. "I'll bet your mom was proud of you, huh?"

"Maybe." I bit my lip. I didn't think Mama was ever very interested in my artwork. Maybe when I was little. "She used to tape my pictures to the refrigerator," I mumbled, tipping books off the chair by the window so I could sit and look out at the tree. "It's stuck all over with pages from the twins' coloring books now."

Robin and I didn't speak for the longest time, as if being so seriously sad had shocked us into shyness. "I just can't believe what happened to your mom," she said. "It's so horrible!"

I stared at two squirrels in the branches.

"And did Richie really take her to the hospital in his car?"

The squirrels ran down the tree trunk and out of sight before I got the lump in my throat swallowed so I could answer. "It was Jimmy's idea. Dad and anybody else who could drive were gone. Jimmy went and begged him to come, and he did." I could see Richie's house through the leaves, enough to tell that only his old man's pickup was in the driveway.

"Wow." Robin's voice was soft. "Who would think that Richie Scudder would do such a good deed?"

When I didn't answer, when I just kept my back to her so she wouldn't see me trying not to cry, Robin came and put her hand on my back. "You okay?"

I knew that she wanted me to talk and talk and tell her about Mama and everything that happened and what it was *like,* but I couldn't.

"You wanna be by yourself for a little bit, huh?"

I nodded my head, not trusting my voice.

"Everything will work out," she said. "I mean, it has to, doesn't it?"

"Maybe." But I didn't see how.

* * *

Almost all of our first momless day, when neighbors weren't visiting us, Daddy was in the boys' room, talking to them or crying along with them in Larry's under-the-bed hiding place. Sometimes Georgie bounced on the balls of his feet, screaming and flapping his arms as if his body couldn't hold how mad he was, and he didn't want anybody but Mom to touch him.

Jimmy and Clark helped me scrub the kitchen some more.

"Why can't we go to the hospital and see the baby?" Clark asked me.

"Dad said maybe tomorrow."

"Well, anyway," Clark went on, "who's going to take care of us now?"

Good question. I looked up to see my brothers staring at me, like they expected a good answer. Jimmy's lower lip wobbled. "God'll take care of us," I told them, "and so will Daddy."

I tried to remember the Bible word for horrible sadness. *Woe.* They hoped I was right, I could tell, but still, we all were full of woe. It was kind of a relief, right then, to hear someone at the door. Miss Lillian and her

124

sister were looking in through the front door screen. "Knock, knock!" she called. "May we come in?"

"Yeah," Clark answered. "You can!"

Sad-faced Miss Effie handed him a bowl covered with aluminum foil. She put her hand on his head. "Poor little fella."

Clark frowned up at her. "Thanks, ma'am. What's in here?"

"Potato salad, youngster. Made special just for you." Miss Lillian turned to me. "Honey, Oscar told us about your loss, and we feel so terrible."

"Your mama was a mighty sweet woman," Miss Effie added.

"Now these are my Hungarian Meatballs," said Miss Lillian, "for your daddy and you children. Just warm these up." She set a heavy blue bowl in my hands. "Serve 'em with some noodles or rice and open up a can of green beans to have alongside. You can take your time getting this bowl back to me. Now I'll write you the recipe if you like."

"Thank you, ma'am. You're both real nice." I gave her and her sister each a small smile. "I'll bet this is good."

I put the bowls in the icebox and went back to my scrubbing. It took my mind off needing to know how to make food besides Jell-O and melted cheese sandwiches, which just scared me all over again. And it was better than being upstairs helping Aunt Bevy choose which of Mama's dresses to take to the funeral parlor.

"You all need to be with yourselves awhile," she'd said. "And I've got to check on Trixie and get us organized if we're to stay over here with you all." Aunt Bevy was going to be here? Relief must have showed on my face. She winked at me.

Jimmy sat up straight. "You're going to bring your dog over here?"

"Yup, you'll have me and Trixie to contend with for the next couple of weeks. I've got some vacation time, and I already fixed it up with my boss. Think you Cathcarts can stand us?"

"I guess so," said Clark, wrapping his arms around her waist.

Dad walked Aunt Bevy out to her Volkswagen. "Thanks, Bev," I heard him say.

We had the Monroe ladies' food for dinner. It was good. "Except," said Harry, "we're not very hungry, Daddy."

"Just eat what you can, son."

We had Mr. Herman's pie instead of the birthday cake and candles we'd planned on.

"So Carmen and the new baby have the same birthday?" Clark asked.

Oh man.

I shuddered at the thought of sharing my birthday with the person who ruined it. The twelfth of July would be—I lay down my fork and pursed my lips tight—Mama's deathday, too, from now on till forever, thanks to this . . . this uninvited baby. Dad reached over and squeezed my hand. With his other hand, he covered his eyes for a moment. "Listen, you kids. For one thing, we'll need to get our Sunday clothes all pressed and ready for your mama's funeral . . . uhm . . ." He cleared his throat. "Well, let's say *ceremony*."

Jimmy leaned his head on Dad's shoulder. "That's a better word."

"It's set up for day after tomorrow." Dad blew his nose in a big blue hankie before he went on. "And two is that you all have a baby sister over at the hospital." One by one, he looked at blubbery Georgie and the teary twins, tight-faced Clark, the top of Jimmy's bowed head and, for the longest time, seemed like, at me. "You all might be tempted to hold what happened to your mama against that little girl when it's not her fault."

My eyes met Jimmy's when I felt his staring at me.

"It's going to be all our jobs to raise up this little child," Dad went on, looking at each of us. "We'll need to give her an extra dose of love because—"

"Because she won't have Mama," I finished Dad's sentence for him. I couldn't look at him, though. It'd be too sad.

"She's a Cathcart, just like the rest of us. We . . . well, we just gotta make sure she knows what a sweet, gentle mom she had." A sob forced its way into Dad's words, and two tears of my own slipped out and slid down my cheeks before I could stop them. We were just a bunch of quiet sniffling until Dad said, "Enough of this!"

He smacked the table with his hand and made us all jump.

"Come on, you kids. Let's go get in the car."

"Where we goin'?" Clark asked.

Harry and Larry echoed, wiping their eyes and noses with the backs of their hands, "Yeah, Daddy, where we goin'?"

I looked over at Jimmy and Clark exchanging

glances, looking awful anxious.

"To see the baby!" Dad sort of tossed these words over his shoulder as he snatched his keys off the nail and stomped out the door.

Jimmy kind of sleepwalked while the others scrambled into the station wagon.

I hung back. "I'll just stay here in case more company comes."

"No, this is important, Carmie. Hop in." Dad held the door open and motioned me to sit in the front seat where Mama always sat. My insides got even jumpier. Dad shut the door. I looked at my fists in my lap.

"But Dad," Jimmy asked, "will the hospital people let us see the baby?"

Dad tapped at his wristwatch. "It's only seven. It ain't like visiting hours are over."

"Yeah, but Daddy," Clark asked, "will they let all us little kids visit?"

"I'd like to see them stop us."

I hoped they would.

Nine

In which one goes out and another comes in
through the hole in the world.

The hospital people didn't exactly want to let Dad take all of us kids up to where they kept the babies, but I guess we all looked so pitiful, they had to give in. They pointed us down a couple of hallways. Georgie cried because Dad wouldn't let him press all the buttons in the elevator. The ride turned the bats flapping around in me into little dragons. A broad-faced nurse named Marjorie walked up to Daddy and had him sit in a green plastic chair. She put a pink-wrapped bundle about the size of a ten-pound sack of C&H sugar into his arms.

"She's just been fed," said Nurse Marjorie. Because

she knew what a sad family we were, tears glittered in her eyes. Daddy's pale, weary face opened like a flower when he looked down at the bundle. The boys clustered in to look at this little pink *it* that had caused all the trouble. I sat down far enough away to avoid looking at the baby, but close enough so people wouldn't think I didn't want to.

"Can I hold her?" Jimmy asked.

"Sure." Carefully, gingerly, Dad handed the baby to him. "Support her head, now, see?" As soon as Jimmy got his hands on it, he stood up quickly enough to startle Nurse Marjorie and came over to plunk himself down next to me.

Okay, she was pretty. Like one of those baby flying-piglet angels from the Botticelli book. Her violet-petal eyelids popped open, and she looked right at me. The color the cornflowers took on at dusk down at Blue Top: that's what her eyes were like. She pursed her lips, poked out her tongue. A spit bubble sparkled on the tip of it.

Did she have any memories of Mama? Or of heaven? Did she know she'd ended up in Missouri and was stuck with us Cathcarts now? Ha-ha, baby, lucky you.

My hand reached itself over to her.

Her cheek was soft. Jimmy put his head on my shoulder. She wrapped her fingers around my pinkie and, instead of her bawling, like babies do all the time, I was the one. Even though I was on guard against being a crybaby in front of everybody, especially strangers like Nurse Marjorie, I couldn't help it. My head bowed until I felt soft, pink blanket against my forehead. The baby stuck her tiny, slobbery fingers in my hair and I about drowned her probably with hot, quiet tears. Jimmy put his hand on my back.

On the way home from the hospital, Dad stopped and bought a newspaper. He showed us where all our names were printed in it.

INDEPENDENCE EXAMINER
SATURDAY, JULY 13, 1963
<u>OBITUARIES</u>

DOROTHY LOUISE CATHCART, 37, Independence, died Friday, July 12, at the Independence Sanitarium. She was born February 25, 1926, in Lexington, Mo., to Hubert M. and Ruth E. (Smith) Brown, and was a lifelong resident of Missouri. She was a homemaker. Her survivors include husband Eugene Cathcart, daughters Carmen and Velvet Elizabeth, sons James, Clark, Harold, Laurence, and George, of the home, and sister Beverly Gillespie of Kansas City, Missouri.

Visitation will be held from 3 to 4 P.M. Monday at Speaks Chapel.

Graveside services will be held at 5 P.M. Monday at Sibley Cemetery.

Sibley Cemetery was the graveyard by the river, the one where we'd left the flowers for Mama's folks. Would Grandma and Grandpa be glad to see her? Maybe they'd want to know how Life had been since they left it and thank her for the peonies every year? I wished we didn't have to go out there, but going to the funeral home was going to be even worse.

"I am not too little," Clark growled at Aunt Bevy. He pressed his lips tight over his big front teeth.

"Okay then," she said, giving in. "Fine with me if it's all right with your dad." Clark could go to the funeral parlor with Dad, Jimmy, and me. "But Georgie and the twins are much too young, Gene, to see—well, too young to . . ."

Aunt Bevy was the one who wasn't up to seeing her little sister laid out in a casket over at the funeral parlor. I could tell from the way her hands shook getting her Lucky Strike lit. "I've arranged everything with the undertaker," she said, "so if it's all the same to you, Gene, I won't come to the visitation."

"It's fine, Bev."

Aunt Bevy gave Dad a grateful look. "I've . . . well, I've said my good-byes. I'll just meet you all out at the cemetery." Then she turned her face away from us.

I wished I could get out of going either place. In spite of Harry's howling to come with us, Dad agreed with Aunt Bevy. She'd find dry pants for Georgie, drag Larry out from under his bed, and meet us at the graveyard. Daddy parted and slicked down the boys' hair and his own while I searched for socks that matched. As I ironed my navy blue dress with the white polka dots, Clark and Jimmy tucked in their chins, watching Dad's big fingers tie their neckties.

The funeral chapel was lined with rose-colored curtains. Behind them somewhere, a record player was playing the slowest, gloomiest hymns in the book. Dad gripped my hand hard the minute we saw the casket. My eyes fled from the sight of the polished Box and its open lid, but seeing a muscle twitching in Daddy's lean jaw, seeing where he'd cut himself shaving, seeing him bite his lip and square his shoulders before he went over to where Mama was: these were almost worse.

Some dressed-up strangers, a pastor and his wife from the church nearby, walked up to us. They shook Daddy's hand and mine. "We stopped by to pay our respects, Mr. Cathcart. We read about your loss, yours and your children's, in the paper and wanted to, if you don't have a church home, invite you to ours next Sunday." Dad's chin trembled as he nodded his thanks to them. They bowed their heads over Mama for a minute and went away.

The undertaker's nametag said "Frank Beeler." He had some light hair around the edges of his head, but the rest of it was like a tanned, freckled egg. His black suit was rumpled and his eyes, magnified by his glasses, were brown and kind, like dogs' eyes. Mr. Beeler shook hands with all of us but Clark, who'd gone right up to the Box.

Me, I studied the flowers. I sniffed at a green glass vase full of red and yellow zinnias with a couple of white carnations and a card. Under the silver-printed "Sympathy," Mr. Herman and each of the Monroe ladies had signed their names. There was a bouquet of roses, too, from Aunt Bevy. Just when I was thinking it was nice for Robin's family to send a big bunch of foofy, rocketing gladiolus, Clark's high voice sort of sliced right through me. "Her hands are cold!" he said, standing on tiptoe, reaching inside Mama's coffin.

Jimmy wanted me to go up there with him, to be beside Clark and Dad—and Mama. I didn't want to, but I had to admit it was true, what Jimmy'd whispered: "It'll be our last chance to see her, won't it?"

It felt like a million miles, but of course it was only a little bit of carpeted floor between me and my mom. I folded my arms tight and chewed the inside of my cheek. Seeing her there, the way she was—it'd mean believing that she was really dead, wouldn't it? I took a step, then another and another, then there she was in front of me—and yet, not there at all.

She had on her sky-blue dress, the color of her home now. She lay in a bed of pink satin. You could tell that her eyes had been glued shut and that her freckles had been powdered over. There was a kind of pressure in my head and heart, pushing hard against the dam holding back my tears. But falling apart in front of everybody was—no. I did not plan on doing that. Not when I saw tears fogging up Jimmy's glasses or when Daddy bent down to press his wet face against Mama's powdered cheek. Then Mr. Beeler walked up to the Box and, without a sound, he closed its lid down over Mama's cold, calm face. I hurried away from everybody and out the door.

Outside, for everybody else in the world, it was a regular old summer afternoon. I wiped my face with the palms of my hands and breathed in big gulps of air. I had to be calm, had to make my heart quit banging, before everybody started coming out of the funeral parlor for our cemetery ride.

"Carmen?"

"Oh man!" I gasped, startled, squeezing Robin's hand and swallowing hard at the tears in my throat.

"Mom said I could walk over here if I came right back home and not bother you guys on such a, you know, such a family occasion." Robin glanced at the big glass doors. "Should I come in and—see her? You know, say good-bye to your mom?"

I shook my head. I couldn't say it out loud, but no, she was too late. I pursed my lips. No one could see my mom, not ever again. The lid was shut. We heard an engine start up and Dad saying, "You boys get in the car. Now where's Carmie?"

Robin hurried with me for a few steps until the sight of the hearse stopped her. "You better go," she said, and gave me a quick hug. "See you later."

She stood watching, holding her hand up, waving her fingers up and down at us, as we began following after Mama in the big black hearse, off to the grave-yard.

When we got there, my eyes went back and forth from Mama's coffin to the boys' and my dad's faces. I looked at the marker on Grandma's and Grandpa's graves. I saw Sarah Somebody's angel stone, the one I'd made the rubbing of. A redbird swooped from tree to tree in the late afternoon sun. Mr. Beeler, the undertaker, nodded his shiny head to us. Aunt Bevy bobbed her head at him and the black polka-dotted veil of her funeral hat floated around her sorrowful face.

Was Mama's spirit looking down from the sky? Was she invisible beside us?

"Look, Carmie," Harry whispered, pointing at a very long earthworm squiggling out of the freshly dug hole in the face of the world. Then Clark nudged me and looked off to the trees by the rusty old gate at the edge of the graveyard where, not even two months ago, I'd seen the old lady. Richie Scudder lifted his hand to us. Then he and his old Cadillac left a dust-bomb trail up the gravel road. We didn't see him again for a long, long time.

I wished I could drive. I'd go where no one could find me, like to the ocean. Anywhere as long as I could go, all by myself, *away*.

When it was getting dark, our folks let Robin and me go up in her tree. It was too sad in our house. We stared up into the leaves over our heads and listened to the grown-ups visiting over on our porch. We could smell Mr. Herman's pipe, Aunt Bevy's cigarettes, and something unfamiliar.

"My dad smokes cigars sometimes," said Robin. "Not in the house, though. Mom won't let him."

Our eyes widened at the clinks of bottle caps being skipped into the street and at the sound of soft singing. Old churchy songs about flying away and the "sweet by and by." Mr. Culpepper's voice was very low, deeper than Daddy's. They sang, "Hard times, hard times, come again no more."

"You okay, Carmen?"

"I guess so. Well . . . not really." How I *really* felt was rotten. Maybe when I died and went to heaven, the guardian angels would toss their pretty hair, rustle the clouds with their wings, and explain to me why they didn't—or couldn't—keep this crappy, train-wreck-of-a-deal from happening to Mama, but meanwhile, I had to figure out how to live and not be mad for the rest of my life.

"At least you still got your dad," Robin said.

Well. Sort of. Except he seemed like people you see on the news sometimes, who are in a war or just had their houses burned down or turned into splinters by an earthquake. "And you got your aunt," Robin went on. "She's so neat. She'll be a good help, won't she?"

"I guess so," I replied, but I figured that she and I both knew that even a really good dad or aunt didn't make up for a mom, not when you've always had one.

If only I could point Robin's flashlight through the leaves and shine it on Mama, sitting on the porch swing. If only we'd come into the kitchen tomorrow morning and there she'd be. . . .

Did she say anything to you?" There was just

enough light to see Robin's anxious face. "I mean, your mom—you know, at the end?"

My fingers fumbled with the wrapper on my Three Musketeers, as I remembered Mama's words. "She said for me to look after the little ones."

"Wow." Robin shook her head and mumbled, "My mom would probably say keep your bed made and don't get too fat." She bit into a Hostess Cupcake. Off down below, Dad and the others were singing about Jeannie and her Light Brown Hair.

I missed Mama, but there was something else. Something too embarrassing to say even to myself. She was up on the other side of the stars, counting on me to help Dad take care of all my little brothers and the new, helpless baby. She was up in heaven, but I was stuck down here, *without a mother.* It made me want to howl and holler and bawl worse than even Georgie ever could. I put my hands over my face. Wouldn't I be ashamed—wouldn't I be such a pantywaist to worry who was going to take care of *me?* Just when everyone was going to expect me to be so responsible? What, was I some big baby who wanted her mommy? That's just what I was. And dumb, too, I told myself, stupid not to think all of these thoughts until now. I sat up and whispered it a few more times: "Stupid, stupid, stupid."

"Carmen?" Robin touched me. "What's the matter?"

Maybe it was like what Jimmy said once, about Dad sticking his arm out the window while we were driving. "I read in this science book that if another car knocked your arm off, you wouldn't feel it at first," and Dad said, "That so?" That's what happened to me: my mom got torn away and now the *real* bad feelings were coming. I scrambled to the edge of the platform, too jangled even to be scared of the rope ladder.

"Where're you going? Be careful, you nut! Don't fall!"

"Oh Robin," I said, sounding like someone who just realized she left the bathtub running, "I just thought of some stuff. I'm all right, honest." Liar. Scaredy-cat, stupid big baby, liar. "I'll talk to you tomorrow, okay?"

Robin's worried face looked over the edge of her tree house. "Okay."

Her mom poked her head out her door. "Oh good, Carmen, I was just about to call you girls down out of there. What a terrible time for you, dear. You're in our prayers."

I told her thanks and hurried through the black shadows cast by the Culpeppers' porch light, across the yards and driveway, past the sad grown-ups on the porch.

"You okay there, Buddy?"

"Yeah, Dad." Sure. Right. Everything's wonderful.

From her place on the porch swing, Aunt Bevy called out, "You goin' to bed, honey?" She flung her arms out at me. "Well, give us a kiss!"

I had to get through all of the hugging, the nighty-nights, the sweet dreams, and say your prayers before I could get inside the house. Maybe I'd dream about my poor mom in a kitchen full of blood, and my eyes caught on Mama's rocking chair in the dark front room. I could say a million stupid prayers, but still the chair would be empty in the morning. Up I went, two stairs at a time, my thoughts spinning faster now that I was alone to think them.

At least Aunt Bevy was going to be here for a while. I knew she wasn't cut out to look after a houseful of kids but still, how were we going to manage after she and her poodle went back to the city? And who was a million jillion times less cut out to be a substitute mom than my aunt? *Me*. Carmen Cathcart, who never, ever even got asked if she wanted to be a big sister, much less a motherless girl left holding a bagful of kids to take care of! And what made it even worse was that if people knew how I really felt, they'd say I was mean and rotten and selfish and—oh man, I could feel it way back inside of me: a runaway river of tears. And no matter how hard I tried to stop it, it was going to sweep me over the cliff into a forever of babysitting, into my permanently momless life.

I was almost to the top floor when the sounds of voices stopped me. In Jimmy's room, Clark was saying . . . what Darren's mom told Mr. Culpepper about us when she didn't think he was listening. She said how our poor dad could ever look after that bunch of rowdy kids all by himself she didn't know. We're not rowdy! And besides, wasn't that rotten for her to say that, about us not getting looked after?"

I moved closer. "Yeah, well," said Jimmy, "I'm not so sure myself just how we'll get along."

"Carmen will help take care of us." Clark sounded hopeful, and I sank down onto the steps.

"She'll try," I heard Jimmy say, "but she's just a kid too. Plus she's not very interested in us."

I bowed my head and put my hands over my ears for a couple of seconds before I made myself get up and stomp the rest of the way up the stairs, wiping my nose with the back of my hand. "Hey, you guys," I said, faking normal. "It's after ten o'clock, for crying out loud. Go to bed."

I grabbed Tiny Tears off my bookcase and curled up with my old doll. The window fan and my pillow kept anyone from hearing me cry. I had to, a little bit, or I'd bust. How could we live without Mama? What were we going to do? Not even a week ago I was just worrying about going to the movies on my dumb birthday. Jimmy was right: I was just a kid. How was I going to survive eighth grade in a new school *and* help take care of a bunch of little brothers and a helpless, tiny, bawly baby sister?

"G'night, Jimmy," said Clark; then he gave my door a thump. "G'night in there."

I didn't—couldn't— say anything, just got my crying under control, just listened to Clark's footsteps on the stairs. Old house creaking. Water rumbling in the pipes. Away downstairs, Dad and Aunt Bevy telling our neighbors good night. Mice skittered through the walls behind all my angels, princesses, goddesses, and my made-up Sarah Somebody. They all stared down at me, Carmen Cathcart, who was going to be a real artist someday. "Stupid," I whispered to myself. I heard a door close downstairs, and our house was quiet—except for the sound of somebody else crying besides me.

I found my flashlight under my bed and padded into Jimmy's room, shining my light on crumpled corduroys and stacks of books. It was like a messy owl's nest. I didn't want to cheer him up by tripping over an encyclopedia or a pile of *National Geographic* magazines. He'd cut animal pictures out of them and stuck them on his walls. My light lit up the face of a lion, lots of dogs, and monkeys. I sat on the edge of Jimmy's bed and put my hand on his back.

"Go away."

"You're not the boss of me," I said softly, but he didn't answer me. "We'll be okay. We've still got Daddy. And Aunt Bevy will stay with us a little while."

"I'm not crying about that," Jimmy's muffled voice said.

"Well, what then?"

"You don't even know."

"I would if you told me," I said.

He turned over. With tear streaks and without his glasses, Jimmy looked kind of soft, like when he was little. "You know what she said?"

"Who?"

"Mom, dummy!" He wiped at his eyes. "In Richie's car. At the hospital." He sniffed and used a corner of his sheet to wipe his nose. "She held my hand really, really tight and I could tell she was scared, so I told her that she'd be okay and I yelled for Richie to drive faster. Then Mama said if something happened and if she—" Jimmy inhaled a big breath.

"She said it'd be extra hard for you 'cause you're the oldest, plus being a girl.

"She hurt really bad, so it was hard for her to talk, but she . . . it was like she knew things were going wrong and she had to say everything really fast just in case—in case she couldn't ever talk to us again."

A fresh wave of misery swelled up inside me.

"She said, 'Carmen loves us really,' but you like to be in your own imaginary kind of world, away from everybody, just drawing pictures and stuff, like maybe you're kind of . . . well, selfish sometimes."

"She said that? You're making that up!" Or the little

147

goon just didn't hear right. Mama couldn't have said that.

Jimmy sniffed. "Oh, I don't know; it was just so horrible, that's all. And Mama said it'd be hard for me, too, because real life was harder than books, and we'd both have to help Daddy, because it'd be the worst for him. She kind of whispered for all of us to be nice to each other, then it was like she fainted, and I was so scared."

I hugged him like Mom would as he cried and talked about how, at the hospital, "they took her and put her on one of those rolling things? And she woke up a little bit, just when they, the nurses, were taking her away. Mom said, 'Be a big boy and take care of the baby.'" Jimmy sobbed. "But how can we?"

Like I knew. I felt pretty hopeless and my head hurt, but at least I wasn't the only one who was scared to death. I felt sorry for him and tried to think of something cheerful. "Abraham Lincoln was only about your age when his mom died," I said, stroking Jimmy's hair. "That's just for you to know."

"He looks pretty sad in all of his pictures," Jimmy said sleepily.

"We'd better get some shut-eye, huh?"

"Okay."

I smoothed his sheet up over him and went back downstairs. I found me an aspirin in the medicine chest and Dad in the little boys' room, gentling Harry out of a nightmare. "Shush now. There now. It's all right now," he whispered. Dad looked like he'd walked a thousand miles and he smelled like Budweiser. He settled Larry and his stuffed rabbit into his bed. I led Georgie to the bathroom and back to his bottom bunk bed, a soft little cave with Clark and Aunt Bevy's poodle both snoring up on Georgie's roof. Dad was arranging the noisy window fans to blow on the boys so maybe he didn't hear Georgie call me "Mommy" which, I'll bet, would have upset him pretty awful. It did me. I didn't let myself go all boo-hooey or anything though, in case Mom was watching over us. I wasn't going to act like some selfish ivory tower crybaby and make Daddy feel even worse than he already did.

When he hugged me and asked again if I was okay, I nodded. He cupped the back of my head with his big hand. I did like he did for me when I was little: petted his back and said that things were going to be all right, to make him feel better. It didn't have to be true.

I began to understand that when it comes to comforting, it's better to give than to receive. That way you can stay in charge.

As I flopped onto my bed, our clock chimed way off downstairs. Before it got to the twelfth ding, everybody in sad, crummy old Cathcart Castle was asleep.

PART TWO:
AFTER

Ten

In which Dad brings home the baby,
Aunt Bevy loses her sense of style, we have company,
Velvet and I make our acquaintance.

It was late, after nine o'clock the next morning, when I went downstairs. I figured Aunt Bevy'd be there, but it was still a shocker, seeing her in Mom's kitchen, cracking eggs into a bowl and stuffing slabs of Wonder bread into our toaster. Trixie was wolfing down poodle food.

"That all you're gonna have?" Aunt Bevy asked Clark. "Those Sugar Pops?"

"Uh-huh."

I crept away from the kitchen door as a wave of lonesomeness swept over me. Momsickness. I went to sit in her rocking chair. All of the things that Jimmy said last night about Mama, what she'd said, everything that had happened, and all of my worries were still boiling around in my mind. How could everything be so wonderful, like it was on my birthday, then be so stinking hopeless?

I sighed. My head was stuffed with troubles, but, I was realizing, my stomach was empty. I walked back into the kitchen. Breakfast, at least, was a problem I could solve. I'd just have to be like one of Mama's junky closets. I'd sort myself out later.

"'Morning, Aunt Bevy," I said. "Where's Dad? And Georgie and the twins?"

She turned around, leaned up against her sinkful of rubber nipples and baby bottles, and squinted her naked eyes at me like she had a headache. She dug into the pocket of her pink bathrobe for a cigarette. She poked it into her unpainted lips and fired it up just as Jimmy walked into the kitchen.

"Hey, the car's gone. Where's Dad?" Then he frowned at her cigarette. "You're not going to smoke those things around the baby, are you?"

If she'd had her eyebrows drawn on yet, we'd have seen them frowning at us through her smoke. Aunt

Bevy pursed her lips, gave a ladylike snort, and poked her cigarette into the dishwater to hiss and die.

"Good morning to you too," she said. "The little boys had their Cheerios and went to play in the back-yard—" She turned to look out the window, then rap on it with her knuckles. "Where Larry appears to be pinning a dead squirrel up on the clothesline by its tail.

"The factory gave your old man a few days off, you know. I sent him to get powder and formula for the baby, some groceries for the rest of us. The doctor called and said we needed the baby worse than they did so maybe your dad would like to stop by the hospital and give her a ride home." She stopped to sip some coffee and blow her nose. "Now judging by the skunk eye you all are giving me, I reckon you all miss your poor mother and, to make things worse, you have to see me without my war paint, huh?"

"You look real nice," Clark said, around a big mouth-ful of Pops. She patted Clark on the head, smiled at Jimmy and me. "Sit down. I'll feed you. What do you want?"

"Scrambled eggs?" I suggested, buttering myself a piece of toast.

Aunt Bevy set about fixing eggs, sipping coffee, and

talking. "Now we have lots to do to get ready for the baby. Keeping busy will keep our minds off our troubles. Only the calendar can fix them."

"What's that mean?" Jimmy asked, looking up from his Cheerios.

"It just means you'll feel better and things'll work out as days go by."

I sure hoped so.

Aunt Bevy started outlining a chore campaign like she was a general and our house was a battlefield. "All of us are going to give this place a good going-over," she went on. "We don't want your mother looking down from heaven and seeing us all going to hell-in-a-handbasket and not giving that baby a good start. Clark, you head on up and get to picking up toys. I want to see the floor of that bedroom of yours."

"They're Harry and Larry's toys too," Clark grumbled.

"I'll send 'em up," Aunt Bevy agreed. "I don't want those little knuckleheads setting fire to the neighborhood, messing around the incinerator. I'll get it going, then it'll be your job, Jimmy, to take care of these piles of papers and magazines pack ratted all over this place. I'm sure your dear, sweet mother always meant to set a match to them as soon as she got around to it." Jimmy and I traded astonished glances as Aunt Bevy wrinkled her nose at a cardboard box full of musty, mousy-smelling diapers, baby clothes, and blankets.

"Carmie, you know how to work that washing machine in the cellar?"

"Sure." With the toe of my tennis shoe, I nudged the box down the cellar steps. I was shaking out tiny duds and poking them into the machine when I heard a bunch of stomping and voices.

"Carmie, Daddy's home!"

Our old washer was thumping and spinning so I couldn't really hear Clark hollering at me. It was one thing to meet a baby at a hospital when she was so cute and I was so emotional—and I could hand her over to Nurse Marjorie and leave. Sure, I could tell myself it wasn't the baby's fault that my mom was dead. It was a whole 'nother thing to have it here in the house.

"Look at that red hair!" Aunt Bevy's loud, hoarse voice came through the ceiling beams. "Why, she's just how Dee looked when she was a baby!"

"How old were you then?" Larry asked. I found out I could hear better if I stood close to the furnace vent.

"Six going on seven."

"That's our age!"

"Carmie!" Harry called from the top of the steps. "Come up and see the baby! She's so cute!"

"In a minute!" I waited awhile, then I sneaked upstairs and out the back door without anybody seeing me. I pinned a bunch of teeny wet nightgowns, diapers, and things to the clothesline, then, as quiet as I could, came back in and hid behind the kitchen door.

I could see and hear Dad telling Larry, "Support her little head now. Don't let it wobble. And be careful about that spot where her head bones aren't glued together yet." Georgie stroked her fuzzy hair.

Okay, okay, I didn't blame the baby for ruining all our lives and everything. Still, I found lots of other things to do besides go look at her. I cleaned my room. I stayed up there, reading "Babies: Care and Feeding" in the B encyclopedia while everybody else took turns admiring the baby as it took turns sleeping, crying, eating, peeing, and you can guess what else. Later that afternoon, when the Culpeppers came over, it was this last thing that helped me to feel a little better about the baby. I thought it'd look too suspicious if I stayed invisible when Robin was visiting, so I came downstairs, feeling pretty bashful and uncomfortable in my very own house. Dad shot me sort of a worried look as Robin bent over him to exclaim over the baby in his lap.

"Ooh, look at her little fingers!"

So he wouldn't worry about me being too sad or mean, I gave Dad a lopsided smile as Robin went on sweet-talking. "She's so pretty! Oh, look at her pink booties!"

"Her aunt bought 'em over at her store," said Dad. "Did they have a sale, Bevy? I swear, this baby's got booties in every color there is!"

Smiling Aunt Bevy shooed Dad's question away as she accepted a bulging pillowcase from Mr. Culpepper.

"Here are some things of Robin's," he said.

"Why, thank you!" Aunt Bevy crowed. "Aren't you so thoughtful!"

"We weren't sure you'd have much for baby girls," said Robin's mom, eyeing all my brothers. "And Robin outgrew these things years ago."

Robin and I rolled our eyes at each other as Dad told Old Yeller Culpepper how kind she was.

"Now tell me again," she asked me, "what's the baby's name?"

"Velvet Elizabeth."

"How unusual! May I hold her?"

Three seconds after she was in Mrs. Culpepper's arms, Velvet made a pretty unmistakable sound. The boys smothered giggles with their hands.

"Her face is all red!" Darren marveled.

"She's pooping!" Harry cried.

We all laughed or smiled a little, for about the first time in three hundred years.

Even Robin's cranky mom chuckled as she held her out to me. "Here, Carmen, you better take her." I froze. Mrs. Culpepper didn't know this was a big fat surprise for me. She didn't know I'd never held this baby before. It'd be bad not to reach my arms out.

She felt soft and sort of solid in my arms. Warm, too, like a cat, except she was a person. I bit my lips and my face felt hot, with everybody looking at me, even Velvet. Her faint eyebrows puckered into a frown. She was my sister, all right, my only one. I choked out the only thing I could think of. "She's heavier than I thought she'd be."

"Eight pounds, two ounces," said shaky-voiced Dad. "Nineteen inches, stem to stern. You want me to take her, Buddy?"

"No, I got her."

Aunt Bevy blew her nose and Mrs. Culpepper said, "Well, we'd best be going."

"That's a swell baby you got there," said her husband. "Robin, you and your brother stay if you like. Pay attention to that diaper business—it'll be educational!"

All the time I was changing her, Velvet stared at me. Her serious expression didn't match her rubbery kicking legs. Just like her soft skin and perfect, teeny fingernails didn't seem to go with the icky *stuff* in her diaper. The boys giggled, and Dad handed me the diaper pins when I got to that part.

"Don't stick her."

"I won't." The minute I got her baby powdered and pinned up snug into her diaper, Velvet shrieked and flapped her arms. I couldn't help smiling.

Robin grinned. "I guess it feels pretty good to be clean when you've been all poopy in the pants."

From the look on Clark's face, you'd have thought I was handing him a radioactive horsepie when I gave him her diaper. "Go rinse this out and put it in the diaper pail, pretty please."

With his thumb and exactly one finger, he held the dirty diaper as far away from him as his arm would reach.

"We want to see that baby," said Mr. Herman and

the Monroe ladies through our front door screen. Miss Effie squinted her eyes at Georgie's wall scribbles, then at the soda straw castle hanging from the *Sputnik* chandelier. She breathed a soft "Hoo-eee!" to herself.

"You got a right homey house here," said Miss Lillian. She picked Velvet up and cradled her. "I can't think when I last held me a baby. You're just the sweetest, prettiest little peach I ever saw! Yes, you are!" All goo-goo-boo-boo, the way people talk to babies.

Mr. Herman touched the baby's hand with one of his long, trembling fingers. He peered at us through his spectacles, inclined his head in Velvet's direction, and announced, "This little child is come to teach you all about life."

"That's the Lord's truth," said Miss Lillian, and Miss Effie nodded as she reached over to give Harry's hand the lightest little touch. "Honey, a big boy like you doesn't need to be doing that," and darned if he never sucked that thumb ever anymore.

We *were* in terrible trouble, but, as Robin and Jimmy and I watched Miss Lillian cup the rosy palm of her old hand around Velvet's head, I thought maybe we weren't completely doomed.

* * *

"Are you guys enrolled yet?" Robin was helping me hang diapers on the clothesline. "My mom and dad said to ask you and if you weren't, they'd help you do that."

"Would they really?" I looked over a row of towels at her. With everything there was to do and get used to, I was glad that our first days at school were still more than a month away. Still, it was like knowing trolls were waiting for us to come down the road.

"Maybe," I said, "I'll be so nervous I'll have a heart attack on the first day of school and not have to go."

Robin giggled. "Is your aunt still going home next week?"

"Uh-huh. I knew she couldn't stay very long, but I'm still kind of scared about her leaving. She said she's out of vacation, plus all the fall hats were coming in at her store." I mimicked Aunt Bevy's foghorn voice: "'Don't think I won't be checking in on you, honey. You'll all just take it one day at a time. If I don't go back to work, they'll fire me, then Trixie and me *would* be in a fix!'"

Robin and I traded glances over a row of jeans, not even having to say out loud how weird grown-ups were. "I gotta go practice my piano," she said.

"See ya later," we promised each other.

For a long minute after she disappeared into her tidy house, I stood out in the yard. The bedsheets on the clothesline—the way they moved gave me a good idea for a picture: a lady in a long white gown, running in the wind. . . .

"Carmen!" Aunt Bevy poked her head out the back door. "You wanna come in and get Georgie out of my hair and down for his nap while I give the baby a bath? She spit up all over both of us!" So I didn't draw the lady in the white dress right then because I didn't have time, and I didn't later on because life without Mama to take care of things made me too tired.

I wasn't the only one.

Our momless life had pretty well messed up our stylish aunt. After a week and a half with glum, messy Cathcarts plus an insomniac baby, her clothes didn't match anymore. She'd taught Jimmy and Clark how to iron their own shirts and me how to make spaghetti plus other foods that wouldn't poison everybody, but it was a whole, new, frazzled Aunt Bevy who stomped over to see who had the nerve to ring our doorbell. Yapping, barking Trixie went too, along with some of the boys, plus me holding fussy Velvet. We all were surprised to see Mr. Beeler, the undertaker, standing on the other side of our front door, whipping his brown hat off his speckled head.

At first he looked worried, then like he was smothering a smile. "I'm sorry, uhm, Miss Gillespie? Have I come at a bad time? I'm Frank Beeler—from the funeral home? We spoke when you made the arrangements for your sister. I know I should have called first."

Aunt Bevy's hand followed Mr. Beeler's eyes up past her unpainted face, up to her hair curlers. For a second there, she looked like she'd just seen her very worst school picture printed in the newspaper.

"No, you're fine," she said, recovering. "Come on in, won't you?" We all made way for Mr. Beeler as Aunt Bevy grabbed Velvet, who'd stopped crying, out of my arms. "Carmen, let me take that baby. I'll run get her— something . . . ," she said, hurrying into the kitchen.

"Uh, Mr. Beeler," I said, "you want me to take your hat? You wanna sit down?" Before he could say anything, our aunt reappeared with her curlers hidden under a scarf and pink lipstick on her mouth. Velvet's had a pink pacifier plugged into it.

"Is there a problem, Mr. Beeler?" Aunt Bevy asked. "May I get you a glass of tea?"

"Uh, no! I mean, no, thanks, there's no problem. I apologize for, uhm, barging in on you all like this. You all were on my mind, your tragic circumstances—I was concerned about you and . . . your family." He glanced down at his shoes. "I—I just thought I'd stop by."

Aunt Bevy smiled at him. "Why, that's very kind of you, Mr. Beeler."

Some radar in my head told me that this might not be the last time he'd be checking up on us. Sure enough, he called us on the phone the very next day and asked Dad if he might stop by, maybe bring us kids a treat. When he did, Aunt Bevy made sure all her makeup was on and that her hairdo was perfectly perfect.

Late that night I was out on the porch with Velvet. Both of us were trying not to sleep and waiting for Dad to come home from work. "Don't you think it's weird," I asked the baby, "that Mama's undertaker came to see us and brought us Popsicles? And aren't you worried about Daddy? So tired and gloomy? And crying sometimes, by himself in his bedroom, Clark says, and not even trying to laugh at his goofy jokes. Dad didn't used to be like that, trust me."

Only that morning, Jimmy and I caught Dad slamming cupboard doors in the kitchen, muttering to himself, "Damn this hard-luck house" and how he'd "never shoulda come here." It made me even more worried about us Cathcarts. Velvet spit out her pacifier.

"And I'll tell you what else, Baby: I didn't used to be all sad and nervous and sleepy all the time, either, not until you came along." I stifled a yawn as I poked her pacifier back into her mouth. "It's just that I can't sit and draw or read or anything . . . no offense. I know it's not your fault."

You can say anything to a baby. No cussing, nothing ugly that might seriously warp it, of course, but babies (1) make good listeners, (2) they won't tell anybody what you said, and (3) it's a good way, Jimmy said, to teach them how to talk your language. Whether it was Spanish or Swahili, it'd still be Earth talk and foreign to babies, since they're all new immigrants from heaven.

"You were up there just a little while ago," I went on while she gnawed on the knuckle of my index finger with her little pink gums. "I wish you could talk while you still remember what it's like and say if the angels warned you that you weren't gonna have a mom." Darned if Velvet didn't start whimpering: first sign of a storm of baby bawling.

"You know what I'm saying?"

I think she was starting to understand English and life-forms on our planet. She squawled like the dickens when it came time for Aunt Bevy and Trixie to go back to their city life. "She must know you're leavin' us, Bevy," said Dad. "Find her a clean pacifier, will ya, Harry?"

I folded my arms across my chest full of worries. They scurried around inside of me like lizards, while weeping Aunt Bevy hugged the teary boys good-bye.

"It's not as if I'm going to Mars, for heaven's sake! You know I'll be calling every day and be here every Thursday on my day off—you'll be sick of me!" She kissed the top of my head. "You'll do fine," she said into my ear. "You're a brave girl." Not true.

We waved until her car disappeared around the corner, then Dad, holding crybaby Velvet, turned to look at us. "Now you kids quit your cryin'. Velvet's doing enough for the whole town. Jimmy, tell me, do we have a roof over our heads?"

"Yeah." Jimmy sniffed.

"Carmen, look at me. Do we have food to eat?"

I nodded my head. So did Georgie.

"Clark, do you kids have a dad who's gonna take care of you?"

"Uh-huh," said Clark, and Velvet's crying settled into ordinary fussing.

"Yes, Daddy," said Larry.

Dad's eyes were real bright. They looked like blue sparks were going to shoot out of them any minute. "Fine then, let's all show a little backbone," he said as he walked past us. "Come on in the house, now. Supper's on the stove."

Eleven

*In which I count down the oogly-boogly days until school,
Mr. Beeler has a question, the Monroe ladies have an adventure,
and maybe I have a dream, maybe not.*

If Mama's spirit was keeping track of us or any other
ghosts or angels were hanging around Cathcart Castle,
they'd mostly hear a bunch of me hollering things like
"Larry, bring me a diaper!" and "Jimmy, quit reading your
dumb book! Do I have to do everything around here?"

They'd shake their heads at Jimmy and Clark and
me trying to cook. They'd hear giggly, grimy boys calling, "Car-mie!" all the time or the little ones bawling
and sounding like what you'd get if you crossed a fire
engine with a jackhammer. And Dad's warnings, tossed
over his shoulder as he plodded off to work in the

afternoons, then me on the porch calling, "You boys
come in now!" at blue nightfall. Remembering to say
"Who's there?" before we let Robin or one of the other
Culpeppers come in and hold the baby, look around,
ask us if we were okay. Or Mr. Herman, loaded down
with peppermints and jigsaw puzzles. Or one of the
Monroe ladies carrying a good-smelling bowl of something and saying, "We just made too much of this; won't
you help us eat it up? We'd be glad to show you how to
make this recipe."

I hope it made the angels happy when Dad took us
to church on Sunday. The pastor there looked happy to
see us, sad, then happy again, remembering us Cathcarts
from the funeral home. I put a nickel in the offering
and told God thanks for not letting things be too gross
our first week on our own.

The first day of school was thirty-three days away when
Aunt Bevy came over on her next day off with a load of
school supplies.

"I checked the lists in the paper," she said. "I think
I got almost everything you kids are gonna need."

"Wow, thanks!" Harry cried as he and the other boys
ripped through crackling sacks of tablets, binders, pencils,

yellow boxes of Crayolas, Pink Pearl erasers, plastic-wrapped slabs of notebook paper, and flat, black tins, each with a brush and eight squares of color. They reminded me of a picture I'd seen a long time ago, of a painter in a magazine. His watercolors came in tubes. "He's a real artist," I'd said to Mama.

Aunt Bevy's voice came into my memory. "Gene," she said, "you gimme that baby. Georgie and I will watch her while you take the kids to get signed up."

When I told Dad that Robin's folks offered to help us kids get enrolled, he snorted. "That was real neighborly and kind and I'll tell 'em thanks, but I'm not such a pitiful pantywaist that I can't get my own kids situated."

The boys waited in the car while Dad and I found the office at the junior high and I got my class schedule. It gave me my first good hope since Mama died: Sixth hour: Art. Teacher: Mrs. Montisano. Not just a "Clear your desks, children; get out your scissors, construction paper, and paste" grade school art class. This was junior high! A *real* art class— my first. I was almost not as scared about school starting. Almost.

* * *

More than a week went by before Daddy had time to take me to the store to get my art supplies. He frowned at my list. "What's a 'crow quill'? You gonna draw with a bird feather?" he wondered.

"Oh Dad," I said, like I knew.

"Well, hurry up and pick 'em out, Buddy. I gotta get to work."

A crow quill was a tiny steel pen point. We bought one and its plastic holder along with the rest of the things on Mrs. Montisano's list: a bigger pen point, its wooden pen holder, and a bottle of India ink to dip them in. Sticks of charcoal, and a sandpaper pad for sharpening them and the drawing pencils. A special eraser wrapped in cellophane, a ruler, a compass, and two paint brushes. I ran my hand across the smooth pad of thick white paper and a bigger one of newsprint. If I didn't have to get supper on the table, I'd have opened each little jar of tempera paint right then. Having all those art supplies was like having perfumes and diamonds in my dresser drawer. I checked the calendar: twenty-three days before I could start using them. My insides fizzed.

Downstairs the worried-looking kids were frozen in front of grandpa-voiced Walter Cronkite on the TV news, right in the middle of their coloring, reading, diaper changing, and clay play.

"You know what he said?" Jimmy asked.

"What?"

"President Kennedy's little boy died!"

"You know, their new baby," said Clark. "Isn't that rotten?" He went back to tugging pink plastic pants up over Velvet's fresh diaper.

Jimmy scowled at the TV. "It's like it doesn't matter if he was a little baby or someone's a good person and didn't do anything wrong. It's not fair, Carmen!"

"Mom would probably say that life's just real good and real bad all mixed up together," I said.

"I guess," said Clark, "we just have to get used to it, huh?"

"That's what Daddy would say," said Larry.

Three days later was Velvet's one-month birthday. Mr. Beeler showed up on our porch again and pulled a pink bunny rabbit out of his pocket. "For the baby." Either because of the bunny or Mr. Beeler's green aloha shirt, Velvet made a happy whooping crane sound. For an undertaker, he sure was colorful—and flustered.

"I was wondering," he said, "Mr. Cathcart . . . and

you children, of course, if it would cause you all any offense . . . uhm . . . if it would be all right if I saw your aunt—Beverly, I mean—socially?"

Dad's mouth twitched and his tired eyes lit up. "Why sure," he said, rubbing his angel wing tattoo. "If it's okay with Bevy, it's dandy with me." He and Mr. Beeler looked at us kids. "Fine with you guys?"

Velvet gurgled. Jimmy, Larry, and I nodded our heads. "Heck, yeah!" said Harry. "You got any Popsicles this time?"

Georgie started bouncing. "I want one!"

Clark cocked his head to one side and frowned up at Mr. Beeler. "You and Aunt Bevy are gonna go out on a date?"

I couldn't wait to tell Robin about this!

"You know what he did? He asked all of us to go get hamburgers and root beer with him and Aunt Bevy. Wasn't that nice?"

Still, Robin and I couldn't help giggling at Mr. Beeler's idea of a romantic date.

The other kids went with Dad, but Clark and Velvet and I got to ride in the back of Mr. Beeler's Chevy. Velvet's eyes were big in her little baby head. It bobbled and turned against the palm of my hand as she took in the lights and sounds of riding through town at night. She had a teeny taste of soda pop and, thanks to Clark, she and Mr. Beeler got to hear about me getting peed in the eye by baby Harry.

When school was ten days away, Aunt Bevy brought us bulging bags of school clothes from her department store.

"You're too good to us, Bev," said Dad, shaking his head as he zipped up Georgie's new jeans.

"Oh, pish posh," Aunt Bevy replied, holding a blue sweater up to me. "I was sure this would be your color. Wasn't I right?"

I nodded at our reflections in the mirror. "Thanks. It's real nice."

Aunt Bevy handed me a blue plaid skirt. "Go try this on now," then she started talking to Dad about every charming thing Mr. Beeler had done, every funny thing he'd said. Before she drove away, she waggled her red-tipped finger out her car window at me. Maybe I was looking like I was thinking of about ten million other things besides telling her good-bye. She squeezed my hand and squinted up at me through her flashy sunglasses. "Carmen? Are you really all right, honey?"

"I'm okay." I wished people wouldn't ask me, especially all soft like that.

It made me too emotional.

She pursed her red lips. "I don't think I've seen you really have a good cry, not once, since this all happened."

"I have too," I defended myself. "You just haven't seen me, and besides, it doesn't do any good."

"I'm not so sure about that."

I pulled my hand away and gave her enough of a smile so she could leave and not feel bad. "Anyway, so long. And thanks for the neat clothes and everything."

But I guess my worries still showed on my face because Aunt Bevy still looked like she was sad for me, but shoot, if your mom dies, then you're not *supposed* to be all okeydokey, are you? She gave my hand a squeeze and drove away as I waved her good-bye. I hoped it made Mama feel a little better about being dead, looking down and seeing that her sister and other people were helping us live, even if we *were* kind of living like a person walks after he's busted his leg: with a limp.

* * *

Nine days till school.

Robin pulled Larry and Georgie in the wagon while I carried Velvet up to see the Monroe ladies. Miss Effie smiled and put her garden-gloved finger to her lips. She and her sister looked from us to each other, then to the radio man reading news about a "march on Washington." Miss Lillian switched off the radio as soon as he was done.

"Whew, you kids got good timing," she said, plopping into a lawn chair. "We need to sit down. Give me that baby!"

"We brought back your bowl," said Larry. "Carmen put cherry Jell-O in it."

"Why, thanks!" said Miss Effie. "I better get this in the icebox then."

She whisked into the house and back out again as Robin was asking Miss Lillian, "Are you excited about all those people going to Washington?"

Miss Effie nodded. "Lillian and I've been talking about it all morning, thousands and *thousands* of all kinds of folks marching right to the government's front door."

"There'll be speeches, singing, and I don't know what all," her sister added, "about making this the free country it's supposed to be." Miss Lillian tilted her head this

178

way and that, frowning down at the baby in her lap, holding Velvet's feet in her hands. "There might be trouble. But then, it might be the chance of a lifetime," she said, like she was arguing with herself. Then Miss Lillian looked up sharp, like she'd come to a decision. "Effie, why don't we go?"

"What?"

"Why don't *we* go to Washington?" The sisters looked at each other for a minute, like plenty of consideration was fizzing behind their faces.

"Yes," said Miss Effie, "let's do. I believe we should."

Not very much later, we were trailing after the boys clattering the wagon down the sidewalk. "That's how I want to be when I grow up," said Robin, "just like those ladies: decide just like that"—she snapped her fingers, making Velvet blink—"what big, exciting thing I'm going to do or what amazing place I'm going to go to!" She reached into her pocket and flicked her yo-yo out and up.

I walked along, cradling Velvet in my arms, and felt kind of bad. I wasn't like Robin. From where we were, I could see Dad in our yard, waving at us, carrying his lunch box for work. Today, anyway, the future was just hard and scary, that's all.

"Carmen? You okay?"

"I wish people'd quit asking me that," I snapped.

"Hey, I'm just being your friend, all right?"

I instantly felt rotten, crabby, and guilty for hurting Robin's feelings.

"I'm sorry," I said, touching her arm. "Honest. I take it back. I was just thinking about stuff."

We traded okays and smiles, promises to see each other later, making sure everything was nice.

Eight days.

Robin, Darren, and all us Cathcarts stood outside with Mr. Herman to tell Miss Lillian and Miss Effie good-bye. They were all spiffy in flowered hats and matching dresses: one wide and pink, one narrow and yellow.

"You two sure look nice," Clark said, and got the top of his head smooched.

A taxicab was going to take them to the station, then they'd get on a bus that would carry them to the nation's capital.

"Maybe you'll be on television," Jimmy said. "On the news!"

Mr. Herman looked worried. "You two look after each other. There's an awful lot of trouble these days, you know, between whites and colored folks. . . ." His voice trailed off.

"Maybe you'd better not go," I blurted, letting everybody see what a worrywart I was about everything.

"Not go?" Miss Effie exclaimed. "What a notion!" Even the cabdriver looked at me like I was cuckoo.

"Carmen, do I have to tell you, of all people, that sometimes you just gotta *act* like you got courage and some gumption?" Her white-gloved hand squeezed my fist. "*Do* what you gotta do and you'll *be* brave. You and old Oscar here, you need to be more optimistic!"

"So long then, you two," said Mr. Herman. "Give my regards to Reverend King."

"You better know we will," Miss Lillian said as the taxi pulled away. "You watch for us on the TV!" she called out the window, waving back at all of us.

Mr. Herman came over to watch for them with us. It wasn't an easy job! The Monroe sisters were part of an enormous crowd of people who'd come from all over the country to gather around the Lincoln Memorial on the 28th of August, "on account of America not being fair to everybody," said Jimmy. He held the baby close to the television. "Look, Velvet. See that statue? Just for you to know, that's Abraham Lincoln, the sixteenth president of the United States. That's where you were born. That's your country now."

What if, I imagined, the statue of Mr. Lincoln came alive and slowly got up off his big stone chair and stood up and stretched up tall and taller?

Then I looked up from my laundry folding and saw how, sometimes, real life was as neat as what I could imagine. There was the Washington Monument. On our little black-and-white screen, it sort of looked like a gleaming white toothpick at the end of a long shine of water with thousands and thousands and thousands of people, including Miss Effie and Miss Lillian.

"Hey!" Clark put his head between the TV and the rest of us as he stabbed his finger at the screen. "I think I saw them!"

I tossed a balled-up sock at him. "Get out of the way, Clark!"

"And be quiet!" said Jimmy. "I'm trying to listen!"

Dr. Martin Luther King was preaching to all those people. He reached out his hand and said even though "we face the difficulties of today and tomorrow," he still had a dream for his children and for all of our country.

His words about his dream, the way he said them, knowing our neighbors were there listening, it all gave me that buzzing feeling I used to get when I had a really good picture idea, when I drew and daydreamed of being a real artist someday. That didn't seem very possible now that Mama wasn't here to live out the dream she and Dad had had, of a big family. It was like I had to trade my dream for hers. It made me mad on top of feeling guilty, because it was selfish probably to feel the way I felt.

As these crummy thoughts whirled around in my head, my eyes sort of rested on the soda straw castle, turning gentle and slow in the air over all of us kids. Mama'd called it a different name when Aunt Bevy gave it to us the first night we were here—what was it? Somehow it felt important to remember.

"Will you listen to that," said Mr. Herman, motioning his shaky hand at the TV.

The preacher had stopped and reporters were talking now. Mr. Herman went on, "Imagine Miss Effie and Miss Lillian and all those people there in such a place, seein' all that with their own eyes. And hearing such words."

I remembered then what Mama and Aunt Bevy had said their dad called the straw castle in his diner. "Mr. Herman, what does it mean when someone says 'dream castle in the air'?"

He gave me a startled look. "Well, I don't know . . . people used to say if you go around daydreaming of big things you'll do or have—or be, even—you're building castles in the air."

Jimmy looked at Mr. Herman real sober. "So is that preacher guy, Dr. King, doing that? When he says that about his dream? About America someday?"

Mr. Herman scrunched up his mouth like that'd help him think. "Maybe. Maybe he is. It does seem to me, though, that there was a wise fella who said once if you *had* gone and dreamed yourself up a castle, then what you gotta do is build a foundation under it."

"How exactly would you do that?"

Mr. Herman raised his eyebrows and a corner of his mouth turned up. "Well, I reckon you'd just have to work like the dickens to make your dream, whatever it is, come true." Then he looked over at the television and said, "Say there! I'm sure I saw the girls. That's Miss Lillian's hat, sure as shootin'!"

Clark and the littler boys got up close to the TV.

"Oh yeah! Where? I don't see 'em!"

Velvet twisted around in Jimmy's arms and made impatient noises in her language.

"Oh shucks," said Mr. Herman. "No, no, the cameraman's moved on."

Mr. Herman got me thinking about my artist dream. In Art Class, only five days away, I could still be doing what I needed to do, the something that could make a dream come true, like Mr. Herman said, couldn't I? And couldn't it be a way to still be the person I was, keep the dream I had, before Mama died, and—

"Carmen! Pay attention!" said Jimmy. Velvet was fussing, waving her fists, and arching her back like she'd flop out of Jimmy's arms and go someplace else if he'd only let her. "Take her, will ya?" he whined. "Maybe she's hungry."

I took her.

"Sweet baby," said Mr. Herman, helpfully.

Twelve

In which we go to school.

Four days. Three. Two. Did I sleep even one single hour the night before the first day of school? I didn't think so. My brain was a lit-up gas station by a big highway: open for business all night long. I kept thinking about my old school, where I didn't have to change classes; Janice McFarland; the pink dress Mama made for me when I was six; what I was going to wear tomorrow; Blue Top; the blue-eyed boy I saw at the grocery store.... Richie and his big chromy car ... where'd they go? What if Dad and Jimmy got *too* sad or mean like Richie and his dad did after Mrs. Scudder died? What if Jimmy ended up running away from home? And where was Mama *really*? Did she get lost on her first day in heaven? If I'm late to classes, will I get yelled at? What if I have to be a junior high school dropout so I can help Dad with the kids? *What if*—the alarm clock jangled awake all five hundred toads hopping around inside of me. I sat up, gathered my things, hurried downstairs, my heart pounding. Water cannoned into the claw-footed bathtub. I got myself wet, clean, dry, and dressed in my new blouse and green jumper. I wiped steam away so I could see the pale girl in the mirror, putting on her dumb glasses, scrooging up her face as she untangled her hair and finally gave up trying to braid it. My fingers were shaking, plus I didn't have time; I almost cried, thinking how Mama would've braided it—wait. Was that the baby? I rubber banded my wild, red horsetail and hurried into my folks' room, where Velvet was whimpering and kicking her legs in the air.

I bundled her up in my arms so she wouldn't bother Dad, climbed back upstairs to knock on Jimmy's door. "Hey, in there. It's time." Back downstairs the rest of the boys were sprawled out, feet hanging off their rumpled bunks. Velvet fussed louder, helping to wake up the boys before I went down to the kitchen. It was a good thing she was so little. It only took one arm to hold her. That left me a whole 'nother one to fix Velvet's bottle and pour out cereal and juice for the twins.

"No, Harry, I told you already. I can't come with you; Jimmy'll walk you to your class. Old Yell—uh— Mrs. Culpepper will be your teacher. You know her. She'll be real nice. You're going to be so smart and have so much fun!"

"No, we won't."

"Will the other kids know our mom died?"

"Maybe. Don't worry about it. You're going to make a lot of friends."

"Are we orphans?"

"Only semi-orphans. Quit asking me stuff while the baby's bawling! Hurry up and eat your cereal!"

Bleary-eyed Dad came into the kitchen. "'Mornin', you guys. Carmie, gimme the baby. Jeepers, let's get a bottle in her mouth before she blows her stack—I can't hear myself think! Jimmy, go get me those dry diapers in off the line out back, okay?"

I pounded upstairs to grab my school things and art supplies and back down again, fuming. "Some stupid little brat got into my paint and spilled it on my note-book paper!"

I wrapped wax paper around a peanut butter sandwich and jammed it into my shoulder bag. Dad, holding Velvet and her bottle, kissed me good-bye and slipped me a dollar. "For milk money. Knock 'em dead, Buddy. Love you."

"Love you, too." I kissed Dad's whiskered cheek and sped out the door, Dad calling, "Be safe—and take a breath, will ya?"

I hurried down the steps, up the street, to meet angry-looking Robin up at the corner. "What's the matter?" I panted, still walking, fast, fast, fast, feeling like I'd forgotten something. "You mad at me?" I asked Robin. "Am I late?"

"No. And I'm not mad."

A lie, I could tell by her frowning eyebrows.

"Okay," said Robin. "My mom was just sort of extra-cranky, that's all. Slow down, will ya? We don't have to run!" So we walked along regular and I remembered breakfast: I wished I'd eaten some. Half a block over, turn the corner, up four blocks more, me getting more and more nervous the closer we got to the junior high.

Fine for Robin, I thought. She'd spent all seventh grade in this big brick box full of strangers all talking and laughing at the same time. I blew out a huge sigh. "Okay, Robin, now tell me you've known every single one of these kids since kindergarten."

"Now, now, Carmie," she singsonged before I jabbed her with my elbow. "You're going to make lots of nice new friends."

She introduced me to a bunch of kids in homeroom, but did I know what to say to anybody? Nothing that wasn't stupid. Could I remember anybody's names? No. Except maybe Becky Scott. "Stuck-up," Robin whispered. Randy Flanagan: "Super-good in sports." Jenny Moffat. "Brainiac."

I'd remember Jenny because (1) her locker was next to mine, (2) in spite of all of our moving around, I'd never really met a black person my own age before, and (3) I embarrassed myself by looking once too often at the neat way her hair flipped up and at her glossy penny loafers. Jenny's had dimes.

"What are you staring at?" she asked.

"Nothing—I mean, I—," I stammered, ashamed. "I just like that, uh, your outfit."

Jenny's look said "Weirdo."

Have some dignity, I grumped at myself as she walked away, her flip bouncing, her pleated skirt swishing this way and that. I got through Social Studies and Math, then sped down two crowded hallways full of noisy kids whacking lockers shut, then up a flight of stairs to get to Science. After that would be lunch, thank goodness.

Miss Spurgeon had a big bosom and a plaid suit. She stood by her posters "The Human Body" (skinless, so we could see the muscles and innards) and "Our Solar System," glaring at two late kids until everybody was totally quiet. That's when my stomach growled. Maybe I only imagined that it sounded like a bear waking up from hibernation and nobody noticed it, really. Then I heard kids snickering. I saw Robin covering a smile with her hand and I saw that boy, the boy I hadn't seen since he saw all of us Cathcarts in the supermarket! Oh man. I was so embarrassed.

When sourpussed Miss Spurgeon took the roll, I found out his name: Greg Tuck.

Robin talked about him on the way to lunch. "That Greg is so cute. Had you met him before? You looked like you did."

"It's a long story." But before I could tell it to her,

Robin saw a lot more kids she'd known since before they'd learned how to tie their shoes. In the big, confusing school cafeteria, she had lots to say to lots of friends besides me, sitting there like a dummy, gulping down my sandwich and milk, not knowing what to say to anybody. Still, I forgot about my crummy morning, stupid PE class, and every other horrible thing when I walked into the Art room. I breathed in the scents of fresh paint and sharpened pencils. This was how heaven smelled really, not like lilies or angel perfume, like some people might think.

Mrs. Montisano's yellow smock and the load of pink rouge on her cheeks made her look extra-cheerful. She'd covered her bulletin board with color wheels, pictures of famous artists, and copies of paintings, even my favorite Botticelli goddess looking like naked Rapunzel-on-a-seashell. That boy, Greg Tuck, was studying her, real close.

"Okay, class," said Mrs. Montisano. Greg turned around and grinned the minute he saw my face, then he went and sat at another table with a bunch of boys. My face felt hot as a frizzy-haired girl plunked herself down beside me. "Everybody settle down now." The teacher tapped her table. "This is a still life," she said, sweeping her hand over a pile of squashes and bottles with dried-up weeds stuck in them. I picked up my pencil. Almost automatically, I began outlining a bottle shape, straight, then curved, then straight again, forgetting about everything.

"You'll be drawing all of this later," said Mrs. Montisano, inspiring groans from some kids, "but today we'll just get to know each other. You may not think you can draw, but you'll be surprised, I know you will. And you'll see why art's important. It helps you to see the world better."

As she talked, as I listened and drew, I knew one thing for sure about art: it made my heart *feel* better. I couldn't wait to do every single project Mrs. Montisano talked about: color charts, mobiles, collages—and suddenly, a folded piece of notebook paper appeared under my nose. Under the table, a hand belonging to the frizzy-haired girl was wiggling and pointing. My eyes followed her finger and landed on Greg looking sideways at me. I frowned at him, then at the unfolded note in my lap.

Aren't you the girl me and my mom
saw in the store? You and your family?

**I think your mom was going to have
a baby.
So, did she have it?
My name** ➡ *Greg Tuck.*

I stuck his note in my pocket just as Mrs. Montisano's
red shoes came clicking across the wood floor. And
she was frowning at me! Was this stupid, note-passing
kid getting me in trouble? In Art class? On the very
first day?

"I'd really prefer that you give me all of your attention while I'm talking," she said. Then she picked up
my drawing and her face changed from stern to surprised. "You've been doing this?"

"Yes, ma'am." I'd drawn another bottle and started
in on a squash, liking its bumps and curves. She asked
me my name and I told her.

"Well, Carmen Cathcart"—she smiled, her cheeks
plumping up like apples—"you've got a fine talent."

I bit my lower lip and smiled back at her, too happy
to say anything and not wanting to be dumb with
everybody staring at me—twice in one day!

"But," she said, looking at me, then over at Greg,

"pay attention in class from now on," just as the bell rang and everybody scuffed back their chairs.

I'd worked my way through the crush of kids and out the door when I heard Greg behind me. "Boy, Carmen Cathcart, I thought I was a goner! It's a good thing you turned out to be teacher's pet!"

"I gotta get to class," I said, hugging my books to my chest.

"Well, me too. English. Room 204."

"Health. Room 117!" I had to yell so he could hear me over the kids all around us who had to yell too.

"That's goony Mr. Henderson's class!" he hollered, walking backward away from me—right into a scowling teacher! I sure hoped it wasn't Mr. Henderson's best friend or something. I didn't have time to hang around to see what happened next. I sped down the hall.

At the end of the day, we had lots of stories to share, Robin and me.

"Your day was more exciting than mine," she said. "I hope you weren't *too* embarrassed when your stomach growled in Science class. That was so funny!" Just thinking about it sent her into such a bunch of giggles

195

that I had to laugh too. Then the thought of Miss Spurgeon made Robin serious: "Her class is going to be so hard."

"You got any candy in your pocket? I'm still hungry."

"Me too," she said, digging cherry Life Savers out of her pocket. "It's all I got."

I remembered Dad was waiting for me at home and walked faster so Robin would too. Our feet swooshed through dry leaves, me thinking about Dad having to get to work, Robin thinking about her own worries.

"Boy, I bet my mom'll have a whole day's worth of nagging saved up for me."

Robin started mimicking her: "'After-school snack? No, I don't think so. Dusting, then piano practice, then dinner—are you *really* going to have another piece of pie? You're such a pretty girl, Robin, to be so plump.' Maybe if I was ugly she'd leave me alone!" She made a face at me, a real ugly one.

I couldn't help smiling at it, but I was worried for her. "You and your mom had a fight this morning, didn't ya?"

"Naah." She wrinkled up her nose. "Well, you know, she was nervous, first day of school and everything. She just took it out on me, that's all."

"Anyway, I'm glad I'm not the only one with family problems," I said, giving her arm a squeeze. We'd gotten as far as our street with the empty-looking Scudder house on the corner. "Do you think Richie ran away from home?"

"I wouldn't blame him." Robin snorted as we walked on down to her yard. "You know what Mom said? Why was I getting chunkier every day? She just couldn't understand!" We both gave her tree house a look.

"How come she's never climbed up and discovered your Twinkies and stuff?"

"Oh, she probably just wants something to crab about," Robin said, then she burst out, "You know what, Carmen? At least your mother really loved you. Sometimes I don't think my mom even likes me, not really."

"How could she not? Robin, you're the neatest person I ever met! You're—"

"Carmie, you comin'?" Dad was in the doorway, in his work coveralls.

"Yeah!" I hurried across the yard, calling out a real good invitation as I went. "Come on over later! I'll let you change the baby's diaper or something."

Robin's face brightened. "I'll go change my clothes first. Mom'd have a conniption if Velvet got poop or anything on me."

Velvet, in her basket, tried to follow Dad with her eyes, him talking and moving like a blur through the house. "How'd it go? You do okay? Have any trouble? Meet any nice kids?"

I told him school was fine and yup, nope, uh-huh, as he grabbed up his lunch box and coffee thermos. "You got any homework?"

"A little."

"I made a pot of chili for your supper. I don't like leaving you alone. No, sir, I don't," he said. Head kiss for Georgie who said, "Don't go, Daddy!" Quick cheek smooches for me and Velvet and talking fast. "Daddy's girls. I'm late for work. Don't let me forget to put a quarter under Harry's pillow tonight. He lost his other front tooth and Larry's jealous. Had to fish it out of his Cheerios." He kept hold of my hand in a hard grip all the while he went through his lock-the-door-call-if-there's-trouble drill.

"We'll be fine," I called to him as he backed down the

driveway. I fixed me a quick peanut butter sandwich and glass of milk plus an aspirin for my headache, then hurried up past the loneliness oozing out of our parents' room and up to mine. I got out of my school clothes, into my jeans, then back down to flop on the floor to color with Georgie.

"Tell me 'bout school," he commanded. "I wanna go—when can I? When are the big boys coming home?"

"Right now," I told him. "Can't you hear that herd of elephants outside? Better go see!" Georgie scrambled to his feet.

Clark brought three new friends home from third grade. "This is Mike and Jerry and Edward. They wanna see the new baby," he told me. "Don't touch her," he ordered. "You'll get germs on her."

"Mitheth Culpepper wath nithe," Harry announced, through the gap in his mouth.

"Really?" Now there was a nice, big fat surprise.

"Yeah, she was happy because we're smart already." With both hands Larry jiggled his own front teeth, trying to loosen them up.

"Sounds like you're lucky and she's lucky, huh?" They nodded at me, then held the door open for Jimmy. We all said hi and even Georgie asked him how his day went, but he just clomped past us and up the stairs.

I frowned at Clark. "What's the matter with him?"

"Some kids were pretty stupid out on the playground, asking questions about Mom." Clark's buddies nodded as he went on, "Like how did she die and junk like that." He rolled his eyes in disgust. So did Mike, Jerry, and Edward. Poor Jimmy. "Did kids ask you about Mom too?"

"Not after I socked 'em," Clark replied. He and his friends were studying Velvet's teeny toenails. "I got in trouble, but it was worth it." His buddies nodded again.

The only thing normal in the blurry, nerve-wracking evening full of momstuff was talking to Robin on the phone. "My mom thinks I need to stick around home this evening, and I can't come see you, okay?"

"Okay," I said. "Yeah . . ." and "Okay," I said again as she told me about the piano piece she was going to practice and what her brother, Darren, did. All the time I was fixing bottles and stabbing my fingers at plates, giving boys silent orders to set the table. I told her "bye and see ya in the morning," so I could make the little squirts eat their supper and help me wash the dishes. I cheered up Jimmy by getting him to read to

Velvet and change her diaper.

We visited with Mr. Herman, I made the boys take baths and wipe up all the water they splashed out, I got Velvet to sleep, and I yelled at Larry for popping a balloon and waking her up. So I had to be awake too, and Larry was mad, upstairs, under his bed, probably.

Now we waited, Velvet and me. The clock ticked. It chimed twelve dings for midnight. In my lap she was like a happy pigeon. In her basket she sounded more like a cranky piglet. Then—car sounds, headlights swooping across the stained ceiling, footsteps, key in the lock. "Daddy's home!"

Velvet shrieked and gargled at him, but Dad and I just smiled. He was real tired looking, like he'd spent his evening pushing a piano up a mountain or a cow up a flight of stairs. "Hey, Buddy. Lemme go wash my hands real quick, then I'll take that baby off your hands."

When he flopped down next to us on the couch, I got a nice whiff of sweat, gasoline, and Juicy Fruit. Dad swooped Velvet from my arms and did a quick lean down, putting his cheek against the top of my head. "How'd it go? Didja have any trouble?"

"No, everybody was nice, mostly. Mr. Herman came to visit and play patty-cake with Georgie and the baby.

Did you have to work real hard?"

Daddy was holding Velvet on his chest and nuzzling her. "Naah, it was easy. You better go on to bed now, honey. I'll take over here."

"You want me to do Harry's tooth fairy quarter for you?"

"I'd've forgotten all about it." I held out my hand as he felt around in his pocket. "Don't know what I'd do without ya," he said, slapping a quarter into my palm.

It was almost one o'clock in the morning, already tomorrow, when I stuck the money under Harry's pillow. Parts of the first day of school were neat. Other parts were pretty crummy, but it was a pretty nice day compared to those that came after it.

Thirteen

In which I have trouble getting my homework done.

My favorite teacher, next to Mrs. Montisano, taught English. He looked like an average guy with a white shirt and a big chin. His hair, pants, shoes, his skinny necktie, even his close-together eyes were sort of the same color as dirt, but those were the only dull things about Mr. Fisher. On the very first day, he wrote on the blackboard: "It was the best of times and the worst of times." His chalk moved fast, squeaking and thumping, ending with five loud cracks: two quotation marks plus a period, then he thumped the blackboard with his fist.

"Ladies and gentlemen," he said, whipping around,

"that's the first line of the best book in the world: *A Tale of Two Cities.* Anybody know who wrote it?"

Only Robin, Jenny Moffat, and another kid raised their hands. I just wrote the sentence in my notebook and repeated it to myself because it was so neat. Jenny knew Charles Dickens was the one who made it up. "Correct!" said Mr. Fisher. Robin nodded, like she'd have said that if only he'd called on her. He held up a book and smacked its cover. "Anybody know who's going to read it?"

A bunch of us kids looked at each other and at the book. It was awfully thick.

"We're going to read a lot," he told us. His teeth were kind of yellow, but his grin was wide. "And we're going to write a lot."

Science class was hard; Robin was right about that. "I shall tell you now," said Miss Spurgeon, "that I am a firm believer in homework."

That went for all of the teachers, except Miss Riley, who taught hideous, embarrassing PE. She only believed in clean gym suits, white tennis shoes, and everybody taking part.

My little brothers and the baby didn't care if I *ever* did any homework, but I did. Instead of drawing the view from my bedroom window for Mrs. Montisano or even just lady-doodling for myself or reading *A Tale of Two Cities* and learning about London and Paris in the 1700s, I was stuck in Independence in the 1900s, either putting supper on the table or a Band-Aid on a head. Instead of studying the planets, I was kissing owies. "You still have lots of blood, and anyway that's what you get for horsing around." Or there I'd be, leaning over the baby's crib and praying to God to let Velvet be as sleepy as I was so I could do my math and read chapter three for Social Studies.

"Do you want this?" But Velvet turned away from the bottle I tried to poke into her pink, bawling mouth, milk and baby snot all over her face. Did she want a pacifier? No. A dry diaper? No. A burp? To be rocked? To be sung to? No, no, NO! To have her real mother? Mama'd know how to make you and me feel better. "Sorry, Baby. You wanna just scream and holler until you feel like shutting up?" I guessed she meant yes.

"Look, I'm miserable too, and so sleepy I could throw up, Mama's gone, and I'm gonna get in trouble tomorrow—do you hear *me* bawling? Listen!" I scooped her up. "You hear the car? Lookee, Velvet, Daddy's home—pipe down! You want him to think I'm bein' mean to you or somethin'?"

"How'd it go, Buddy? Did you have any trouble?"

That's what Dad always asked me.

"We got along fine," I'd say, even if it wasn't exactly true. I gave him reports almost every night, if I was still up when he got home. For instance, "The Monroe ladies came over this evening to goo-goo-gah-gah over the baby and tell Georgie how cute he is. Miss Effie read him a book." Mr. Herman liked to walk across the street for a game of Old Maid with Clark and the twins. Some evenings Aunt Bevy brought food, presents, and happy Mr. Beeler with her when she came to check on us. "And Dad, Robin's mom comes to see us too. Jimmy thinks she's spying on us to make sure we're not burning the house down."

"Well, that's nice of her. It ain't much of a house," he said, pushing his fingers through his stiff red hair and looking around the room, "but it's shelter." He brought his hand down to rest on my leg and said, "I sure hate like the blazes leaving you kids alone here every night."

I thought maybe I'd better change the subject. "Did things go good at work?" Daddy puffed out a long sigh, blowing out his lips, like horses do sometimes, before he said, "Well, it ain't like I'm not grateful for the job, but I've had a heckuva night, I don't mind telling you."

One night his coming home woke me. My head popped up, and a little line of drool ran from my mouth to my Science book. I'd promised myself to learn about the Earth's crust and all of its other layers as soon as everybody quit bawling, fighting, and breaking things. Instead, my book was a slobbered-on pillow.

"Sorry, honey," Dad whispered. "I tried to be quiet." He had dark circles under his eyes, and the tired way he walked over to Velvet's basket reminded me of movie zombies until he smiled at the baby.

"Hey, little lady!" he said. "You're not supposed to be awake!" To me, he asked his trouble question while Velvet wondered, maybe, "Why doesn't Dad ask me about my troubles? A diaper pin stuck me. I had to burp really bad. It was pretty in heaven, and nice, not like this place."

"How're you doin', Buddy?" Dad asked me. "Okay?"

"I'm all right." A lie. Junior high had turned into a big fat mess. It'd be too babyish to bother poor, tired Dad about how I was already falling behind and even Harry and Larry were doing better in school than I was.

"How's school then?"

"Fine." It'd be too pitiful to talk to Aunt Bevy or Robin about it. The only time Robin didn't get an *A* was when she got *A*+ and, up until yesterday, I thought only stupid kids flunked tests. I asked Dad, "How was work?"

"Went okay, I suppose."

That gave me a new thought: maybe Dad was lying to me like I was to him.

"Did you guys have any trouble 'round here?"

I shook my head. I lied. "Huh-uh."

Was my math homework done? No. Did I understand the problems? Not even. Mr. Fisher wanted book reports from us before Halloween: "No trick-or-treating for you, ladies and gentlemen, before I have your thoughts on Mr. Dickens's book *in* my hands! Are you enjoying it, by the way?" I was, honest, but I still had 197 pages to go. Even Greg Tuck looked kind of surprised, and Mrs. Montisano acted mad, like she didn't think I was so very special anymore when I didn't get my complementary color chart painted on time.

When I asked Jimmy if he'd made any friends, he just pushed his glasses up on his nose and said, "My teacher told some kids on the playground they should feel sorry for me and try to be nice to me and that I was just shy. I heard her say it. And Clark socked this one kid, bigger than him even, for teasing me." Both Jimmy's face and his voice were mad.

"There's this one other kid who's new, Wally Williams, and I told him extra stuff I knew about Africa, because we were studying it? For him to know and to try and make friends? He just looked at me like I was the dumb one and now I don't think he even likes me. Does that answer your question?"

"I guess so." I punched his arm, friendly-like. "If I said I liked you pretty much, would that help you feel better?"

Jimmy snorted and wouldn't look at me, just kept reading the funnies in the back of the newspaper. I leaned in close to read the front page. There was another story about the four girls who'd died a couple of weeks ago. They were my age, just about, and just because they and their families were black, somebody'd exploded a bomb in their church down in Birmingham, Alabama. Probably just as I was picking up Georgie's nickel for the offering up off the floor and Dad was making Clark stop folding his church program into a paper airplane, those girls were getting killed. "Poor babies," Mama would have said.

I sighed and looked over at our old angel picture on the wall. What if some guardian angels were the dumb ones in heaven, I wondered, and plain old didn't know how to stop awful stuff from happening?

Miss Effie and Miss Lillian looked pretty bowed down in their Sunday hats when they got home from church that day of the bombing. They went straight into their house and pulled their window shades all the way down. And the next day at school, Jenny Moffat was in a real bad mood. After our Math class when I said hi to her, she grabbed her lunch sack, banged her locker door, smacked her lock shut, and walked away like she didn't hear me, all the while I was still trying to remember my combination. It made me feel bad. Then, as I hurried to get to Science, I began to feel worse. I'd covered it fast with my hand, but Jenny must have seen the big red *F* on my Math test. How could she help it? A thought, a pretty crummy one, came into my mind: smart kids treat you different when they think you're dumb. Did I do that, I wondered, when I got good grades all the time?

Two times last week, I didn't know the answer when Miss Spurgeon called on me. What if Robin started not wanting a stupid friend who was sad all the time?

Behind my eyes tears stung, trying to get out and run down my dumb, gloomy face. It was bad enough that Mama was gone and the world was so mean and I couldn't get my schoolwork done, but I felt worried about Dad, more worried than usual. Something he'd said last week—what if he really meant it? He was extra tired and sad, about leaving us by ourselves of an evening and missing Mama. "I don't know, Carmen," he said, sighing and staring down at his dirty hands in his lap. "Maybe we oughta just clear on out of this hard-luck house and go back to the country. What do you think?"

He needed to get his head examined was what I thought. He needed to go soak his head in a bucket, then go take a long nap, wake up, smell the coffee, and be his old self again before we all drowned in stupid gloom, for crying out loud. He needed Mama. Well, join the club, Dad! And now he wanted to move again? That sounded like a solution he'd come up with. My dad: the restless kind. How much more could we stand?

"I think that'd be dumb" was what I told him, and kissed his rough cheek good night. At least he hadn't said anything more since that night about moving away. And I was glad, but then maybe a different school wouldn't be such a bad idea. I sure wasn't doing very good in William Chrisman Junior High. I'd wanted things to be different in junior high and now, I told my glum reflection in the bathroom mirror, I was. "Carmen Cathcart: Semi-Orphan Stupid Kid, that's me. 'Motherless Babysitter Held Captive in a Rotten World.'" I yanked on the blue outfit Aunt Bevy bought for me and twisted my hair into a messy braid. What if I flunked Miss Spurgeon's class? I gulped down a bowl of cereal and grabbed my books. What if I flunked *all* my classes?

"'Bye, you guys," I told everybody, and hurried to meet Robin. What if, when she's a freshman next year, I'm still a stupid eighth grader? In my mind I stomped on this horrid, crawly roach of an idea as we kicked our way through piles of October leaves, Robin and me, on a regular Thursday morning.

"Carmen?" Robin gave my pigtail a yank. "Hey, you look like your brain is about six hundred miles away from your head."

"Huh?"

"You're probably just nervous about the Science test

today. Don't forget: Earth's diameter is 7,926.41 miles. At the equator, anyway. She'll ask how big it is around the North and South Poles too, I'll bet."

I stopped walking, like I'd smacked into an invisible wall all of a sudden.

"There's a test today?" Each of my feet took a step backward from Robin, standing there looking at me, her head tilted, like I had crawdads growing out of my ears. I stepped back another step from just too many troubles. "I . . . uhm . . ." My eyes fell to my scuffed shoes. "I think I forgot something." I looked up at Robin's mystified face. "I mean . . . uhm . . ." I shifted my grip on my Science book and notebook so I could put my hand over my stomach. "I'm sick.

"I can't go to school today," I said, backing farther away from her, from the noisy school up ahead, then I turned and ran down the sidewalk with Robin yelling after me, "Where're you going? You'll be late! Carmen!" I just ran faster and faster, away, away, and Robin kept calling after me, "Come back! Hey! Where're you going?" fainter and fainter.

I turned a corner and didn't hear her at all, just my shoes hitting the sidewalk.

In which I fall apart in front of Andrew Jackson,
and Robin has a good idea. I look for matches.

I didn't stop walking until I found myself looking up at
the statue of Andrew Jackson and his dainty-footed
horse in the shadow of the courthouse clock tower. They
looked off to the far West, right through the Jones store
across the street and all the modern jumble of city
and everything between them and the Pacific Ocean.
They weren't startled at all by the sudden appearance
of a Kansas City–bound bus, pulling up to the curb
behind me.

The door whooshed open.

A sleepy-looking old lady was looking at me out of

one of the dirty windows. I imagined going west and west-er all the way to California, like on *Wagon Train* on television, only on one stinky bus after another, away, really *away*, from home, from tests and trouble and our stupid house full of sad, complicated relatives, farther and farther away with every passing street sign. I could be like Daddy when he was young, hopping a hobo train. The beak-nosed driver drawled, "You gettin' on?"

I didn't, of course. I was too much of a sissypants. Besides, when Daddy took to the road, he was alone in the world. No one was counting on him like they were on me.

I pitied the family that was counting on me. Drawing and daydreaming were what I was cut out to do. Suddenly my knees gave way and I plopped down on the curb in front of Andrew Jackson. All of the tears I'd been holding onto burst through the door in my head. I couldn't stop them.

I missed my mom. As bad as Mama being dead was having my own life so messed up. This was like that place in the Bible, that "valley of the shadow of death." That's where I was now.

I don't know how long I'd sat there crying when a man's voice said, "Here now! Say there, young lady, what's the matter here? Are you in trouble? Do you need some help?"

"No one can," I sobbed as he patted me on the shoulder.

"There now," he said. "There now, what's happened? Can you tell me?"

My sorry life story spilled out of me along with a fresh wave of ugly sobs.

"My mom died and we still got all these little kids I don't know how to take care of. I can't get my homework done and everything's so—so mean and horrible . . . the whole stupid world's so *hopeless*."

The old man offered me a handkerchief, so very starched and folded that it was a shame to blow a nose into it, but I did and calmed myself down a little before I looked up at the old guy. No, he was more like an old gentleman, in his gleaming, polished shoes, his light gray suit and hat. He straightened up and pressed his hands together on the top of his cane.

"That *is* about the worst thing that can happen. I surely remember when my own mother died. And plenty of other terrible times I can think of when it did indeed feel like the moon, the stars, and all the planets had fallen right square on my shoulders." When he paused, I squinted up at his face, which was a shadow against the early morning sunshine. "Is that how it feels to you?" he asked.

That was just how it felt.

"I guess so."

"Well, young lady, you're dead wrong about one thing."

"What?"

He offered his arm as I struggled to my feet. "The world's anything but hopeless."

I dusted off the seat of my skirt, wiped my eyes, and picked up my books. Now I was ashamed and too aware that I'd been bawling in front of a nice old stranger.

"Do you want your hankie back?" It was pretty soggy and wadded up.

"No, I reckon not. Hadn't you best be getting to school?" he asked in a kind voice. He looked around and, seeing a police car over on Maple Street, beckoned it to come over.

The policeman inside greeted the old man, "Good morning, sir."

"Officer, would you mind giving this young lady a ride to school?"

217

"No problem, sir."

Robin and Jimmy would never believe this. I stared at the gun in the policeman's holster, his radio, handcuffs, and everything else that bristled all over the inside of his car. The gentleman in gray touched his hat brim with his index finger and told me not to give up and always do my best.

"That's all anyone can do, young lady. You'll see that time has a way of fixing things." The morning sun glinting off his glasses was the last I saw of him.

Almost.

It was just as well that the policeman was too busy listening to and yacking on his radio because I was still upset, too bashful, and had too much to think about to talk to him. All the way to school, I gripped my books tight in my fists. If ever there was a time to get control of yourself, it'd be when you were sitting in a cop car and facing a Science test after all. I sighed a shaky sigh, honked my nose as delicately as possible into the soggy handkerchief, and tried to feel better. Even if it killed me, I had to figure out how to survive without Mama and prove to her that I wasn't a crybaby. I had to figure out how to get through school and not be dumb, and how to be a good help to Dad. It would be just like him to load us up and move us down the road. That'd be the last straw. Anyway, wherever we went, we'd still be us. Didn't he know that?

I only needed one glance to tell that kids were watching out the windows of their classes when I got out of the police car. The policeman tipped his cap, winked at me, and said, "Good luck, kid." After I stopped by the office, I washed my face and wiped the tear spots off my glasses and smoothed my hair. I leaned forward to press my head against my reflection in the cool, hard glass. Aunt Bevy would have said I'd had a good cry. I just felt . . . still. It was like after a big storm when everything's calm and nice. But there are busted branches all around.

My heel clicks echoed off the lockers on my way to Social Studies. I did the best I could on Miss Spurgeon's test and later, in the cafeteria, my morning was almost worth how rotten it was, getting to tell Robin and a bunch of other kids the details about my ride to school. I saved the sad, embarrassing parts for when Robin and I were walking home.

"Why didn't you tell me you were having so much trouble?" Robin asked me. I shrugged one of my shoulders. Saying would take too many words. Probably because she's so smart plus being a teachers' kid, Robin had a good idea for part of my problem. "Why don't you see if you can drop one of your classes, and take study hall instead? That would give you time to do your reading and your homework at school, wouldn't it?"

We stood on the sidewalk with our heads bent over a much-folded-and-unfolded piece of paper from the pocket in my wallet with a snapshot of Mama and the ticket stub from *Cleopatra*. Robin smiled at my penciled-in teacher reviews.

1ST HOUR ROOM 204 ENGLISH
MR. ERIC FISHER   *NEAT*

2ND HOUR ROOM 237 SOCIAL STUDIES
MRS. JOAN KIRK   *FUNNY*

3RD HOUR ROOM 312 MATH
MR. ALBERT MORRIS   *SERIOUS*

4TH HOUR ROOM 129 SCIENCE
MISS EILEEN SPURGEON   *HARD*

5TH HOUR GYMNASIUM PHYS. ED.
MISS MIDGE RILEY   *NOISY*

6TH HOUR ROOM 216 ART
MRS. JUDY MONTISANO   *NICE*

7TH HOUR ROOM 117 HEALTH
MR. G. B. HENDERSON   *GOONY*

"What about Mr. Henderson's class?" I asked hopefully.

Robin frowned. "That's one you gotta take."

"I know." Sure, I'd been having a rotten time in school lately, but I was smart enough to know what class I'd have to give up. I chewed the inside of my cheek, imagining myself *not* drawing Mrs. Montisano's collections of bottles and things, or making mobiles or swirling fresh paints together to see what color they'd make.

We went on walking while I folded up the paper and put it away and while Robin fished her yo-yo out of her pocket and slipped its string loop on her finger. She went on talking as a snap of red flashed down and up and into the palm of her hand. "I could help you, maybe, with your math and science."

I bumped my shoulder against hers as we walked along to show her how nice I thought she was for saying that. But partly I felt embarrassed: it was gross, having to have help. Another part of my mind remembered about castles in the air, where people keep all the big things they hope they'll be or do someday, like being a real artist. Giving up Art class might help fix my school problem, but it was as if my dream castle was disappearing behind thick, cold clouds.

"Carmie!" Daddy, in his coveralls, holding the baby in one arm, stood by our door. "Step on it, will ya? I'm gonna be late!"

"I'm comin'!"

"Hey there, Robin."

"Hey, Mr. Cathcart," she called.

Georgie came step-together, step-together down the porch steps, then running toward me, his arms in the air. He was hollering, "Carmie, Carmie, Carmie!" instead of watching where he was going or else he wouldn't have fallen down and gotten all hurt and scuffed up. "Shhhh . . . it's okay. Don't cry," I told him, scooping him up and hurrying into the house. "We'll fix it . . . you want Daddy to kiss it and make it better?"

"At least he doesn't need any stitches, thank goodness," Dad said. "Can you get him cleaned up? Get him a Band-Aid?"

"Sure. Just go," I told him, wringing out a washcloth.

"Carmie, no!" Georgie sobbed. "It stings!"

"I'll put the baby in her basket," said Dad on his way out the door. Velvet screamed, and I didn't even notice that Robin had picked up my school books where I'd dropped them. She set them on the porch and probably went home to practice her piano and study volcanoes while I was calming down Georgie and Velvet.

The twins stomped up the front steps and came banging through the door. "We raced Clark and Darren home from school," Larry panted.

"Yeah," said Harry, "and we beat 'em!"

The twins scrambled back outside to cram themselves onto the porch swing with Darren and Clark, then Georgie, too, as soon as I got his owie patched up and kissed.

All the time while I gave Velvet her bottle, part of me was thinking about not being in Art class anymore. It felt a whole lot more serious than just signing up for stupid study hall. It felt like my castle in the air, my artist dream, was lost in outer space. A nice, brave, unselfish person wouldn't mind having to give up her dream of being a famous artist someday, because she loved her brothers and baby sister so much. I wanted to be good and act like I had some backbone, but how? That's what I asked myself, back inside my head while I dished up chicken and noodles and wiped up spilled Kool-Aid.

"You know, that Wally Williams kid is nicer than I thought he was. He makes model airplanes," Jimmy said. "Hey, I'm talking to you, Carmen. You're not paying any attention."

"I am too," I lied.

Aunt Bevy came to see us after supper. "I brought you kids a pie. It's apple!"

"Did you make it?" Clark asked her.

"No, kiddo, I won't go so far as to say that." She handed me a paper sack from her department store. "Here, Carmen. It's just some little somethin'."

She sat down in Mama's chair and, after making sure he wasn't wet or sticky, lifted Georgie onto her lap.

"Thanks," I said. All soft in its tissue paper wrapping was a dark green sweater. I held it up. "It's beautiful."

Aunt Bevy tilted her head to one side. "You feelin' all right, honey? You look kind of puny. Did you have a bad day? You want me to watch these kids a little bit while you go take a bubble bath or somethin'?"

Should I tell her about running away from school and all my other troubles? She'd listen, but so would all of the boys and anyway, what could Aunt Bevy do? I just said, "Wouldja?" and smiled at her, kind of. "I got some math problems to do."

224

"Well, if you'd rather do arithmetic than take a bath." One corner of her ruby red lips curved up. "Try that on, anyway, and let me see how it looks."

Up in my room, just as I'd pulled the new sweater over my head, my eyes lit on all of my lady drawings all around me. Just like that, the idea came to me, what I needed to do. Sure, it was what a brave, bold, serious, smart person would do, but could I? I gave up trying to concentrate on my homework. "Heck," I muttered to myself, "I guess I can do it in study hall from now on."

On a fresh piece of notebook paper, I began writing down all I had to do and be from now on. I'd just finished the sixth thing on the list when Clark came up to tell me that Aunt Bevy was leaving. "She was gonna holler at you up the stairs, but that'd wake up Georgie and the baby."

I came down to tell her so long and good night and thanks again. Aunt Bevy bragged on how nice I looked in the new sweater. "But, Carmie, you really do look awful pale—you sure you're okay? You seem like you're a million miles away."

I shrugged my shoulders. "No, I'm right here."

Way after Aunt Bevy was gone and everyone was in bed, even Dad, it was like the mice and I had crummy old Cathcart Castle to ourselves at last. I read over my list.

1. Tell Mrs. Montisano that you're going to take study hall instead of Art. (Oh man, what was I going to say?)

2. Be dependable. Don't let Mama down.

3. Be brave or at least act like you are, like Miss Effie said.

4. Pay attention to real life, like when Ann Landers in the newspaper tells people they have to wake up and smell the coffee. (I liked the sound of those words and spoke them, real soft: "Wake up and smell the coffee.") That's what you have to do now.

5. Don't daydream all the time.

6. Do your best, like that old man said.

7. Don't think anymore about being
a real artist and maybe being
famous someday. It's dumb.

Okay.

Fine.

I took a deep breath and blew it out hard. At the bottom of the paper I wrote, Carmen L. Cathcart, October 10, 1963, then changed the date to the 11th because it was after midnight and tore the page out of my notebook. I folded it and tucked it into my pocket, and took one last look at all of my pictures as Mama spoke in my head.

I'm counting on you, Carmie.

I snatched a pen-and-inked, long-gowned lady off the wall. Real quick, in case I chickened out or changed my mind, I yanked down every single dumb princess-in-a-castle, flowing-robed goddess, and long-haired, bird-winged angel. I swallowed hard and my shaky fingers froze when they got to the angel with the head-light eyes from Sarah Somebody's tombstone, from the day we were at the cemetery when Mama was still alive. In the corner of the rubbing was the pencil drawing of my imagined Sarah. I couldn't tear them up, the way her and her angel stared at me, but I wadded up all the other drawings and shoved them into the paper sack the new sweater came in.

Tap, tap, tap, then Jimmy's voice: "What are you doing over there?"

"Nothing," I said, leaning in close to the bedroom wall. "Go to sleep." I gathered an armload of drawn-in, filled-up sketchbooks plus the sack of crunched-up pictures, then I tiptoed down the stairs, stepping soft, breathing quiet, down and through the house. Except for the ticking clock and the mice skittering through the walls, everything was quiet.

I found a box of matches by the back door.

I closed my eyes, took a deep breath, and crushed my artwork into the backyard incinerator. A chilly wind blew out more than one match as I held the flames to the crumpled papers, then they flared up bright. I swallowed hard as one of the mythological ladies looked at me, as the brown-burning edge got closer to her face. My own face felt the heat as she glowed, turned black, and vanished into red sparks.

I pursed my lips, gritted my teeth, and felt like a murderer, killing the beautiful ladies I'd imagined and, maybe, burning up a giant part of myself. The smoke drifted up past the black treetops, up to where Maina and the angels were watching.

I picked up a stick and poked it into the fire. I watched the flames crackle and spark, feeling grim and sort of hypnotized, not hearing or seeing anything —or anyone—beyond the brightness, so a little scream got startled out of me when, all of a sudden, someone was talking to me!

"I looked out my bedroom window and saw the fire," Robin whispered loudly. "I thought stupid Darren snuck out to play with matches or something."

"Jeepers, you scared me to death!"

But Robin didn't care. She was looking all shocked and mad at smoke curling out from under a spiral-bound sketchbook. "What the heck—!" She plucked the drawing pad out of the fire, threw it on the ground, and stomped it with her bedroom slipper. "Carmen Cathcart, you are so weird!" She frowned, like I was as exasperating as her goony little brother. "What do you think you're doing?"

I hunched up my shoulders and cupped my elbows in my hands. "They're just my pictures and junk," I said.

"Your drawings? What? You burned up all your

artwork?" Robin put her hands on her hips. "So what gave you the big idea to come out here in the middle of the night and set fire to your pictures?"

I didn't—*couldn't* say anything for a minute. She stepped closer to me.

"Tell me, you nut, and make it snappy, will ya? It's kind of cold out here and I'm—"

"They don't go with my life anymore," I said.

"Huh?"

"Not the way it is now, anyway."

"This doesn't have anything to do with you deciding to quit Art class, does it? Golly, Carmen, just because you're not drawing milkweed pods in eighth-grade Art class doesn't mean you're not going to be a great artist someday. So snap out of it, why doncha, and try not to be so sad all the time."

I felt sort of shocked. This was a whole different way to size up my situation.

It was like Robin was pointing me to look at a teeny, hopeful bit of sunlight at the end of a long, smelly, black tunnel. Like she was telling me to wake up and smell the coffee.

Fifteen

*In which I write a letter, Dad tells a ghost story,
Jimmy and I get mail, Walter Cronkite tells us the last straw,
and there are the best and worst of times.*

I found a box of stationery, a present from Aunt Bevy
to Mama, who'd never opened it. "I guess it's mine now,"
I muttered to myself. With my blue ballpoint pen and
my best handwriting, I wrote a letter on a sheet of the
pink paper, folded it up, and stuck it in its pink envelope.

> Friday, October 11, 1963
> Dear Mrs. Montisano,
> I already went to the office this morning before
> First Hour and told the counselor that I wanted

to take study hall instead of your class from now on. I hope this does not hurt your feelings. I would really rather be in your class, but if I don't start taking study hall on Monday, I will flunk.

Your former student,
Carmen Cathcart

Before Art class was even over, I'd put most of my art supplies into my crumpled lunch sack, my heart pounding every time Mrs. Montisano walked past my table. It took me a while to get up the nerve to hand her the pink envelope and say, "This is for you."

"What is it?" Then, loudly, "Class, start cleaning up. The bell's about to ring."

"Uhm . . ." I looked away from her smile and gathered up the rest of my things. "You'll see."

Greg and some other kids shot puzzled frowns at us as everybody milled around the sink and the door, all noisy and busting for school to be over for the weekend.

"You in trouble?" Greg whispered as Mrs. Montisano's eyes flitted over my note. Her eyebrows furrowed and her lips parted.

"No—well, kind of . . ." I answered him through

gritted teeth, not wanting to see his blue eyes looking at me.

The bell clanged. Mrs. Montisano shouted over the racket, "See you Monday!"

I was going to make for the door with everybody else, but she clamped her hand on my arm. "Carmen—?"

"I gotta get to Mr. Henderson's class."

"I'll write him a note," she said, jerking her head in the direction of her cluttered-up desk. I wished I could run out into the hall. Instead I followed her, her smock billowing out like a purple sail. Already ninth graders, coming in for their last class of the day, were giving me curious looks as I rehearsed what I'd say to Mrs. Montisano. I wasn't planning on what she said to me.

"Carmen, I know about your mother's passing."

Huh?

"The other teachers and I have talked about your dilemma."

They had? My—what?

"Your problem," Mrs. Montisano explained, seeing my frown. "I just wanted to tell you I know how hard this decision must have been for you."

I looked down at the pennies in my loafers. "It was

Robin Culpepper's idea."

"Well, in any case, it shows a lot of character on your part. And Robin sounds like a good friend. You'd better get going now." Mrs. Montisano began scribbling on a piece of her yellow notepaper. "Give this to Mr. Henderson."

"Okay." It'd be too sappy to tell her I was going to miss her. Besides, I was getting a lump in my throat. "Thanks," I said.

She gave me a sad sort of smile. "Will you stop by if you have any art questions?" I nodded. "Tuck your supplies away somewhere safe," she said. "I know you'll use 'em again." I was just about out the door when Mrs. Montisano called out, right in front of all those big kids, "I'll miss you, Carmen. You'll still be my best artist!"

The trees got prettier as October went by and school got better as I was able to get my homework done, but home? In a way it was getting worse. My dad was making me more worried than usual. Mostly he was his regular self, except he never sang anymore. And it wasn't just that he looked extra tired when he came dragging in from work or that he punched his bedroom wall and hurt his hand. Or that sometimes he drank a little bit more beer than a normal thirsty person oughta drink. It was all that stuff put together. I wouldn't dare remind him of that crazy thing he said, about us moving again, but I could tell from his gloomy ways that he was still thinking about it. Jimmy was worried too. He was good at noticing.

"We gotta cheer Dad up," he said, turning around from his sink full of supper dishes to look at all of us.

"How?" Larry asked. Georgie thought we should get him some candy.

"He needs to make some friends," said Clark.

Having a party was Harry's idea.

"Hey!" I patted the little squirt on the back. "That's a perfect idea! It could be a combination party: part Robin's birthday, part thank-you for our neighbors being so nice to us here lately."

"And," said Jimmy, "the other third to cheer up Dad." He'd been studying fractions.

It wasn't hard to get the boys to print and color invitations once I told 'em they could use up my left-over tempera paints. "But don't you guys bother any of my other art supplies," I said, giving Georgie the skunk eye. They were put away, safe under my socks, like Mrs.

Montisano told me. "Harry, you and Larry and Clark decorate the front room, okay?"

"For Halloween or for birthday?"

"Both," I told them.

A grin split Clark's pointy face. "Neat!"

I baked Robin a cake, chocolate, with extra frosting.

"Could you buy some orange candles?" I asked Dad. "But what about a present?"

"Hmmm . . . ," he said. He was chopping onions for the stew he was making for supper. Then he looked up at me. "Oh, I got me a good idea for that."

"What?"

"You'll see." He just wiggled his eyebrows at me and began prying the lid off a jar of Mama's tomatoes. "You better go check on the baby and see what Georgie's getting into."

I asked him again, but he didn't tell me his neat idea until right when it was time for him and me to begin on it. Now he only talked about us straightening up the house for company.

My little brothers taped a bunch of black paper bats to the soda straw castle and made a banner of cutout letters: HAPPY SPOOKDAY ROBIN. All this swayed over and surrounded Robin's family, us Cathcarts, the Monroe ladies, and old Mr. Herman. We filled up our old couch and every single chair we had. Mr. Beeler sat on the floor by Aunt Bevy, but I guessed he wanted to anyway, so they could hold hands and look lovey-dovey at each other.

"Happy birthday, there, Robin," Dad said. He beamed a rusty smile at everybody. "It's mighty nice to have you all here."

I was pretty sure he'd realize now that it'd be horrible to ever move away from all these people.

Mama and any other spirits who might be listening heard about Mr. Herman's young manhood in Philadelphia "when I was a shoe salesman and had to wear a suit every day! Different suspenders for every day of the week!" Mr. Herman, who was taking his turn holding baby Velvet in his lap, used his free hand to snap the stripey suspenders that were holding his old-man pants up under his armpits.

Robin got her dad to tell about his barbershop quartet. "And," she said proudly, "he sings in the choir at church, too."

"You all ought to come hear us on Sunday," said Mr. Culpepper. "I should've invited you before now."

"Oh yes," said Miss Effie. "You Cathcarts need you a church home."

"We go to that church over on College Street sometimes," Jimmy offered.

I told Mr. Culpepper, "We'd like to come hear you sing, though," in case Jimmy had accidentally hurt his feelings.

"My, Carmen," Miss Effie went on, "did you bake this cake?" Then she told us how she almost got married to a baker in North Carolina. "Oh my, he was a good looker in his white coat."

"But he was like a rug, lying all over the place," put in Miss Lillian.

Miss Effie snorted. "He was a charmer, even so."

Before they retired, the Monroe ladies were school-teachers, like Mrs. Culpepper.

"Oh yes," said Miss Lillian, "up in Des Moines, Iowa. I taught high school. Effie there taught the little ones."

Harry smiled up at Robin's mom, displaying his new front teeth. "I think you're the best teacher, Mrs. Culpepper."

Robin and I stole glances at each other, but the smile her mom gave Harry didn't have a smidge of crankiness in it. "It's good of you to say so, Harry," she said. "Thank you."

Darren tugged on Dad's sleeve. "Clark said you used to be a hobo. Is that true?"

"Is that so?" Miss Effie exclaimed. Everybody looked at Dad, especially Mrs. Culpepper, whose eyebrows lifted like she didn't much approve of how Dad spent the good old days.

Dad jutted out his jaw and sucked on his teeth like he does when he's thinking. Then he said, "Well, that was bad times when there were plenty of fellers, some as young as Jimmy here, out ridin' the rails, looking for work to do. We weren't bums, I can tell you." Daddy glanced at Mrs. Culpepper. "I can tell you all a tale from those days, son, a Halloween tale, as a matter of fact. A lot of good stories come out of bad times. Wouldn't you say so, Mr. Herman?"

"That's a fact," said the old man.

"Oh, that's true," said Miss Lillian.

Dad rubbed his eyes and began telling us about the Halloween night "back in '39 out in Tennessee" when he crawled into a boxcar and met an old man named Sam. "He told me a tall tale 'bout—well, you all know the statue of General Andy Jackson on his horse up on the Square, right there by the courthouse?" The little boys nodded, open-mouthed.

"Well, there's statues like that all over the country. All over the world, in fact. That old Sam told me that every hundred years, all those stone and metal horses and riders come *alive!*" Daddy strengthened his voice a notch on the last word. Velvet stirred in his arms. "Those horses go leapin' off their pedestals down into the streets. You can hear them clip-cloppin' and clatterin' 'round town carrying their ghostly riders on a search for each other to make an army. Fight their old battles and smell the gunsmoke one more time. Sam told me they go gallopin' all Halloween night. 'I seen 'em wid me own eyes,' he said, 'back in 18 and 63, in the time of the turr'ble war. I was nought but five year old,' Sam told me, 'but . . .'" Daddy paused for effect, and Mr. Beeler squeezed Aunt Bevy's hand. "Came the dawn," he whispered, "the statues were back on their blocks of stone, each and every one, nothin' to show for the gallivantin' but the mud on the horses' hooves."

Jimmy broke the stillness after the story. "Say, Dad, this is *1963*."

"Oh gracious," said Miss Lillian.

"This is the year they ride." Robin's voice was creepy.

240

"Halloween," said Dad. He glanced at the wall calendar then slid a sly gaze over to me and said, "Thursday night."

"Now that I'd like to see," said Mr. Culpepper as my dad got up and hurried off to the kitchen. Robin's mom's eyes smiled over the rim of her coffee cup at the sight of the little kids' oogly-booglies.

"Hey, Carmen!" Dad hollered from the kitchen. "Turn off all the lights in there!" Which I did, of course, and Miss Lillian said, "Oh my!" as a glowing face floated toward us. "Robin," said my dad, kind of panting, "here's your present. Sorry we didn't wrap it—man, this thing is heavy!"

"Jeepers!" she exclaimed like she'd never gotten a giant jack-o'-lantern for a birthday present.

Right then I was so glad Dad was my dad, even when, later on, he and I had to go calm Larry's nightmares. On the morning after Halloween, Dad got us all up out of bed before school so he could pile us into the station wagon and take us over to where I did all my crying. He showed us the hooves of General Jackson's horse. It was impressive, even though I pretty much guessed that he'd driven by the courthouse in the middle of the night after he got off work just so he could muddy up the statue. I put my hand in my dad's rough hand. I felt sure that he was himself again.

A couple weeks later, right after Clark's eighth birthday, when Jimmy and I came home from school, Dad told us we'd both gotten mail. The person I would be two weeks in the future might have told the person I was right then that the scrawled postcard and the letter were warning bells, but of course, she couldn't do that.

November 15, 1963   Fort Hood, Texas
Hey Jimmy,
I bet you're surprised to hear from me. I went and joined the army. It was real tough at first, but no tougher than my old man. I hope you aren't too lonesome without your mom. I know about that. I gotta go, but maybe you'd like to write me sometime? No one else does. Did you hear that the president's coming here to Texas next week?
Sincerely,
Private Richard D. Scudder,
United States Army

The smeared-pencil return address on my letter said it was from—Janice? From my old school in the

242

country? She wrote it on notebook paper and she drew
an angel in the corner. A pretty crummy one.

November 16, 1963

Dear Carmen,

How are you? I am fine. Some of us
read in the Kansas City paper that a
lady named Cathcart died last summer. I
told everybody that that was your mom.
A bunch of kids didn't remember you
but I did. I wanted to tell you that's really
awful about your mom and I hope you're
okay.

Me and my folks, we drive by the
house where you used to live sometimes. It's
empty you know, and there's a mean, wild
goat there eating the weeds. It won't let
anyone catch it, my dad says. Write me
sometime.

Your friend,
Janice McFarland
(I sat behind you in Mrs. Cameron's
class, remember?)

Sure, I remembered. It was kind of a nice surprise that she remembered me. I figured that Dad would want to know about Blue Top, so I read him Janice's letter. Maybe later, if we survived it, I'd get out the pink stationery and tell her about our first Thanksgiving without Mama.

Aunt Bevy had already called me two times to talk about our plans. "I'll be over there bright and early Thursday morning, me and a fat bird and all the other fixin's. We'll stick him in your oven, Carmen, then we'll work on everything else. I'll bring a couple of pumpkin pies from the bakery and just not tell anyone they're store-bought, okay?"

"I can make pumpkin pie," I blurted into the phone. "I watched Mama do it a hundred times. She used to let me roll out the crust."

"Are you sure?" Aunt Bevy sounded doubtful.

"Sure I'm sure." Kind of a little white lie, but it was important, wasn't it, to have homemade pies for Thanksgiving?

Now it was six days away and the entire idea of Thanksgiving, along with the worst cold ever, made me homesick for Mama and sick enough to be home. Or else I would have been at school on that Friday, the

22nd of November, when the words "SPECIAL BUL-LETIN" flashed white on the dark television screen. Then Walter Cronkite said, so it had to be true, "From Dallas, Texas, the flash, apparently official, President Kennedy died. . . ."

Daddy stood watching, slump shouldered in the center of the room. "I swear, if that ain't the last blasted straw that broke the camel," he said, "I don't know what."

Aunt Bevy and Mr. Beeler came to our house on Monday to watch the president's funeral. I blew my nose and studied the way the First Lady's black veil made shadow slashes across her face.

"There's General Ike," said Daddy, pointing at one of the sad old men on the television, come to President Kennedy's funeral.

"You mean President Eisenhower?" asked Jimmy.

"Yup," said Daddy. "And that there's Harry Truman. I was out in the South Pacific, I remember clear as day, when he became president, when ol' Frank Roosevelt passed on in '45. Shoot, Jimmy, he'd been president since I was your age. Truman was his VP so he had to take over. Told everybody he felt like the moon, the stars, and all the planets had fallen down on him."

Huh? I leaned in closer to the screen.

"I'll bet," said Mr. Beeler, "that President Johnson feels just like that right now."

Oh my goodness. "That's him!" I cried.

"Didn't I just say?" Daddy took a swig of his Dr Pepper.

"No—I mean, yes. He talked to me!"

"Nuh-uh!" said Clark.

"Who?" asked Jimmy. "President Truman? In person?"

"Just a few weeks ago, up by the statue on the Square. He was real nice to me." I told them a little bit about the bad day I had that day. "He told me not to give up and to do my best." Dad bit his lip and shook his head at me. I'd met a genuine president and didn't even know it. His hankie was folded up in my underwear drawer this very minute. The corners of my mouth curved up a bit when I imagined Mr. Truman cheering up Mrs. Kennedy like he did me.

"There's a story to tell your grandchildren," said Aunt Bevy.

"Not havin' any—oh, look at John-John!" I said,

pointing at Mrs. Kennedy's little boy saluting when his dad's casket went by.

Mr. Beeler pulled a hankie out of his pocket, wiped his eyes, and blew his nose. "It's his third birthday today," he said. "Just imagine."

Was President Kennedy just now joining the beginners' class up there? Seeing his little baby who died and greeting the Alabama Sunday school girls? Meeting Mama? She wouldn't even be bashful because, after all, this was heaven. I could imagine her meeting Cleopatra or comforting the president. "Look down there in Independence. I used to live with those people. I suppose they're going to be getting ready for Thanksgiving now. . . ."

By Thanksgiving Eve I was seriously pooped. Even baby Velvet, in her basket in the kitchen, had flour in her fuzzy hair and eyelashes. "Velvet's finally asleep and the boys are watching TV. I'm gonna run over to Robin's and see if I can borrow some, uh, celery," I told Jimmy. "Keep an eye on things, will ya?"

"Okay," he said, without looking at me.

"I got those stupid pumpkin pies in the oven,

but I'll be back way before they're done, okay? Are you hearing me?"

Mr. Nose-in-His-Book gave me an exasperated look. "I said okay." Really I wanted to get out of our kitchen and go tell Robin about almost putting chili powder instead of cinnamon into the pie batter. Hardly any time at all went by, it seemed like to me. I was just helping Robin polish her mom's drinking glasses while we talked about the next book Mr. Fisher wanted us to read: *The Witch of Blackbird Pond*. Just the title made lonely, windy-looking pictures in my head. "It sounds even better than *A Tale of Two Cities*."

"I hope the ending won't be as sad," said Robin.

Her mom came into the kitchen just then. "Carmen? I didn't know you were here. Who's—?" she was asking me when we heard Clark and Jimmy shouting. "Carmie! Where are you! Come home quick! Car-men! The house is burning!"

Sixteen

In which Old Yeller goes too far,
Dad goes nuts, and we go back to the past.

Jimmy was on the front porch holding Velvet in his arms. "I called the fire department already!" he yelled. "Where were you? You said you'd be right back! I called up Dad at his job."

"You *what?*"

"Those dumb pies started burning and smoking and I couldn't put 'em out! And I burned my finger."

"Oh, don't be such a baby! Is everybody out safe?" I hollered back as Robin and I ran into the house. Mrs. Culpepper followed hard after us, shouting about baking soda, yanking down and stomping on a fiery window shade. I was pouring water into the fire flickering out of the wastebasket while Robin flung water on anything that smoked. We heard the siren and the bells. Firemen yelled at us to get out of their way.

Chunks of yellow light appeared up and down our dark street as neighbors opened their doors to see the excitement. Hardly a half hour later, the firemen were rolling up their hoses. Our kitchen was black and Mama's soda straw castle was a soggy, trampled tangle on the living-room floor. The Monroe ladies had wrapped quilts around the boys. Our station wagon came careening through the confusion. Dad jumped out and stalked over to take wriggling, fussing Velvet out of Mr. Herman's arms.

One of the sooty-faced firemen asked Dad, "You the owner? It was just a kitchen fire that got out of hand. . . ."

Dad just nodded, goggling at our dripping, smoky house. I couldn't believe it either. Mrs. Culpepper's tightly folded arms could not hold in all the opinions that started spurting out of her. "Mr. Cathcart, you'll pardon me for saying so, but I've looked the other way, knowing these children were over here by themselves, night after night, with no one but a girl to look after them, but I thought she was pretty responsible even though she was only thirteen." She flared at me.

"I was only gone a few minutes," I put in. "It could happen to anyone!" I hoped Dad would believe that. Stupid. Stupid. Stupid me.

"I'll deal with my own daughter," said Dad. "Now, ma'am, I thank you for helping us the way you have, but that doesn't give you leave to find fault."

"I was determined to mind my own business," said Robin's mom. "I've got half a mind to contact the authorities."

"You'll what?" Dad's voice sounded dangerous.

Robin's flustered-looking mom clasped her hands together. She talked like she was trying to calm herself down and Daddy, too. "Now there's no need to take that tone, Mr. Cathcart. I'm just saying that there are agencies to help people like you. A foster home for the younger ones, temporarily, perhaps."

"Jan!" Mr. Culpepper grabbed his wife's arm. "Now you're going too far."

She shook him off. "I know you've had a tragedy, but someone's got to look after these children properly!"

"Stop saying that!" I shouted, hardly hearing Robin's mom.

"Be quiet!" Dad snapped at me, and he raised his voice to Mrs. Culpepper.

"We're getting along all right! What are you saying—a foster home! You're gonna sic the government on me and my family?"

Mr. Culpepper's deep voice chimed in again, "Now we're all tired—"

"Everybody be quiet!" said Darren.

"Everyone's getting all worked up," said Mr. Herman, but Dad and Mrs. Culpepper just went on getting more upset.

"You're gonna have the government take away my children?" Dad made his voice low again. I'd never seen Dad so mad, and that's saying something. The Monroe ladies raised their hands to their worried faces.

"I never suggested any such thing. I only have these children's best interests at heart," said Mrs. Culpepper. "They all could have been burnt alive and be as dead as their poor mother —"

"Why, you harpy!" Dad exploded.

"And if it wasn't for me—"

"Jan, shut up!" Mr. Culpepper shouted at Robin's mom, and sparks flew out of her eyes.

"Don't you talk to me like that!"

Robin and Darren looked angry, sad, and scared. Dad smacked his hand down through the air like he was shooing everybody away. "Nuts to this!" he growled, and turned on his heel, snapping his fingers at me.

"Carmen, you come in the house with me and help get some things together. Jimmy, don't just stand there with your mouth open. Get your brothers in the car. Put the backseat down so's you can all spread out." He pushed his hand through his wild hair.

Miss Effie said, "Now Mr. Cathcart, you're all upset."

"We'll just bring over some mops and buckets," said Miss Lillian.

"You don't want to be runnin' off," said Robin's dad.

"Dad—!"

"No back talk," Dad interrupted Jimmy and me both before we could even ask where in the Sam Hill Daddy thought we were going. Old Mr. Herman took a couple of steps up our front walk and said to Dad's back, "Now Gene, where you goin' this time of night?"

He and Mr. Culpepper and the Monroe ladies all seemed to be talking at once.

"Mr. Cathcart, there's no need of taking these children—"

"Mr. Cathcart!"

"You can't—"

"Tomorrow's Thanksgiving!"

I had a quick glimpse of Robin's shocked face as I ran after Dad into the house.

"Daddy, you're being crazy!" He flashed a hard look at the mashed straw castle before he stomped on it and kicked an overturned chair. He stalked through the smelly house, listing things for him and me to grab. "I'll get some blankets. There's those loaves of bread and some baloney, and didn't we get a sack of oranges at the store? Bottles and diapers for the baby. Don't forget that half jug of milk—"

"Dad?"

He clattered down the stairs with pillowcases full of clothes and blankets.

"Come on," he said. "Grab that radio over there, Carmie. Let's beat it out of here before God only knows who comes breaking down the door."

He tossed the pillowcases through the Rambler's back window, and I hardly had my car door shut when we were down the driveway and into the street with a bounce. Jimmy and Clark and I looked back at our worried friends and neighbors standing about in the chilly evening, watching us go.

I wedged the grocery sacks full of supplies onto the floor between my feet. Velvet, wriggling on Jimmy's lap, was the only one of us who didn't ask Dad again and again where we were going, but he only had three answers: "You'll see. Everything's going to be fine. Just go to sleep." None of them were any good.

He hushed Georgie, who'd begun crying, and said, "Harry, you and Larry settle him down and take a nap or something."

"We're hungry, Daddy."

"When are we going home?"

"Are you going to give Carmen a spanking for leaving us by ourselves?"

I bit my lip.

"Just curl up and have a little sleep," said Dad. "We'll stop in a while."

Velvet's baby pigeon sounds got fussier as the dark spaces between lit-up businesses and dark houses got wider and wider and we were on the highway heading east out of town. Jimmy, Clark, and I exchanged worried looks. Every now and then, the flare of a stranger's headlights splashed across Dad's thrust-out lower lip, his pointy nose, and the pale knuckles of his two big hands on the steering wheel. In the blackness below the bill of his ball cap, Dad's eyes were twin sparks aimed straight down the long road.

I looked at the glowing numbers that showed how far we'd gone. Ten miles ticked away before I had the nerve to ask Dad, "Is this kind of like when you ran away to be a hobo?"

"Carmen, this isn't anything at all like that."

"Because if it is—"

"I was a kid then and on my own. Now I have all of you and I'm by God not going to lose you."

"But Dad, you're not—"

"No more. Just be quiet now and try and keep the baby calmed down."

I must have slept somehow, or how else could I have woken up the next morning, all shivering cold even if someone had put a blanket over me? My legs ached. When I tried to stretch, my feet pushed against something hard. Where was I, anyway? I opened my eyes and saw a steering wheel in front of my face. It was a shocker to sit up and find out I had the car to myself. I turned my head to look out the window.

If I'd found myself parked in a rusted Rambler in

front of a pointy-towered palace, I don't think I could have been much more surprised. What I did see was a tall, dingy farmhouse and a couple of trees. Behind them was a brown hill which I knew perfectly well would be covered in cornflowers sometime next summer. Dad had brought us to Blue Top.

At the sound of steps rustling through dry leaves, I spun around to see a long, hairy face with large, light eyes separated by a white stripe. I jumped back, bumped my head, and covered a scream with my hand. The pupils in its eyes were shaped like rectangles and, as the head moved from side to side, they both looked in at me through the driver's side window. "Gertie? Is that you?"

Baa-aah, our old goat answered as a sudden knocking behind me whirled me around again the other way. Jimmy was staring at me too.

"What time is it?" I yawned and rolled down the window.

Jimmy checked his Timex. "Almost seven."

A lot of families' moms were sliding fat turkeys into their ovens. They'd be reminding their children to be thankful for their blessings. I *was* grateful that my pies didn't completely burn our house down, but I'd wait and see what was going to happen next before I turned loose any more gratitude.

I opened the car door and climbed out. My blue coat bunched around yesterday's wrinkled clothes. All of me was crumpled. I pushed up my glasses and smoothed my hair away from my face as I stared open-mouthed at our old house. "Why did Dad bring us here?"

"Come on inside and get warm," Jimmy said. "He sent me out to get you. He's making breakfast."

My stiff legs carried me across the yard, up three steps to the slanting porch, and into the house. It still had some furniture: a long table flanked by two scuffed-up church pews. Georgie sat on an old telephone book on one of them. Larry, Harry, and Clark sat on the other, looking like they'd used an eggbeater to comb their sticking-up hair. It seemed to match their bewildered brains, judging by their talk and the looks on their faces.

"I'm going to be a fireman when I grow up," said Harry.

A kerosene lamp stood on a cupboard by the window. I flicked the light switch by the door.

"No electricity," said Clark. Dad had filled our old

258

cooler with most of what there was in the refrigerator back home, then stopped along the way for gas, ice, and a jug of cider. I walked over to the sink in the corner of the room.

"I already tried," said Jimmy. No water.

Velvet waved both of her arms at me from her baby carrier, which sat in the center of the table. She kicked her legs. Dad, who was still wearing his ball cap and coveralls from work last night, stood at the iron cookstove frying bacon and eggs. A dented coffee pot was percolating, so I figured that he'd gotten water from the pump outside. Breakfast smells, at least, were something to be thankful for.

"Good morning," he told me. "I would've had you come inside, Buddy, but you were sleeping so sound there in the car I didn't want to wake you." He didn't exactly seem crazy but, just the same, it was going to take me a while to figure out how our family was in the Thanksgiving episode of *The Beverly Hillbillies in the Twilight Zone*. Why'd I have to show Dad Janice's letter about this place being empty? And why had I ever missed this old farm?

Dad draped an arm around my shoulders. "Hungry?"

"I guess so."

"How 'bout opening up that package of paper plates?"

For now, I gave myself up to breakfast. Time enough later for questions. He knew we had to go back to school on Monday. We knew that he had to go to work.

"Dad, are we going to go back home soon?" Clark asked.

"Yeah, Dad," said Jimmy. "Are we?"

"If it's not too burnt up." Larry flicked his eyes at me. "Our room didn't get on fire, anyway."

"Yeah, Daddy," Harry added, with an enormous yawn, "I don't like sleeping in the car."

"Oh, I don't know," said Dad. "Here's nice."

"No, it's not," said Jimmy. "There's not even anything to read. Why are we even here? And what about Aunt Bevy? I bet she's there right now, wondering where we are."

That really got my imagination going, thinking of the look on Aunt Bevy's face when she and her turkey got a load of our empty, smoky-smelling house.

"There's no television," said Larry. "I want to watch cartoons."

"Me too," said Harry.

Me too, I thought. Dad was really worrying me.

After breakfast he sat back on one tall-backed church bench and propped a foot on the other. He kept a pleasant look pasted on his face as he bounced Velvet on his knee. She wore one of Georgie's knitted baby suits. She laughed and made spit bubbles.

I went to explore the rest of the house. Echoes and boys trailed me up the narrow stairs. The house seemed so different than when we lived here not even a year ago. Of course, what *wasn't* different now? We didn't belong here anymore. This cold, musty place wasn't home.

An empty bird nest rested in the corner of the boys' old room. In the room that'd been mine, I stood where I'd daydreamed away a million hours, in front of a tall cobwebbed window. My hand floated up, so I used my finger to draw in the dust a picture of a long-haired girl. She seemed to be walking up the brown hill beyond the window.

Jimmy, then Clark, and soon the three littler boys were all around me, looking in the closet, flicking dead flies and spiders off the windowsills. Georgie took hold of my hand and Jimmy asked, "What are we going to do?"

"I don't know."

"It's like we're marooned."

Clark told Georgie, "You were a baby when we moved here."

"Like Velvet?"

"Uh-huh."

Harry said he remembered.

"He's still a baby," Larry teased.

"Nuh-UH!" Georgie retorted.

"Let's go downstairs and see what Daddy's up to," I said, hoping we'd find him up and loading the Rambler for our return trip. But no, both of Dad's feet were propped on the bench now. He was singing "'Row, row, row your boat'" to baby Velvet on his lap. "'Gently down the stream . . .'"

"How long are we going to stay here, Dad?" Clark asked. "'Cause we gotta go to school. And you gotta go to work." It turned out that Dad didn't much care if he went to work or if we went to school on Monday.

"But I'll miss my friends," Clark said. "I miss them already."

"We're going to learn take-away next week, Dad," Harry said. "On Monday Mrs. Culpepper's going to read us a new story."

"Don't talk to me about her," said Dad.

"Why not?" Larry asked.

"I like her!" said Harry. "And anyway, I have to go to the bathroom."

"Take me!" said Georgie, looking up at me.

I'd been avoiding thinking about the cold, splintery privy out back. It had been an adventure two years ago when we moved here, but now just thinking about it made me need to do the very last thing on earth I wanted to do, which was to pee.

Okay. Fine.

"Come on, you guys."

Harry put his hand in mine. "Will you wait outside while I go?"

Larry said, "I'm scared of that goat."

All of us but Velvet, who happened to be wearing her personal bathroom, braved the outhouse. Like it or not, we'd gone back in time for Thanksgiving and it was all my fault, mine and those stupid pies.

Georgie held on to me while I helped him with his zipper and snaps. I smoothed his rough hair and shielded him from the wind sifting through the board walls. He asked me, "Is Daddy sad?"

"Yeah, he's real sad."

"He misses Mama."

"We all do, but maybe it's harder for Daddy 'cause they'd been friends the longest, huh?"

"Yeah." Tears welled up in Georgie's blue eyes.

Helping a nervous little kid go potty in a drafty privy in November really helps you to appreciate people who lived in the olden days before some brilliant person invented indoor plumbing. And something about the way Georgie clung to me while I did up his pants made me better appreciate my baby brother.

"They had indoor toilets on the island of Crete in the Mediterranean Sea, two thousand years before Jesus was born, just for you to know," Jimmy informed me when I told him how thankful I would be from now on for being able to go to a nice, regular bathroom. As far as I was concerned, up until there were indoor potties and Thomas Edison's electric lightbulbs, the whole history of mankind was a big bunch of crummy camping.

"How'd you know that?" I asked Jimmy.

"I just do." He shrugged his shoulders, which were hunched against the autumn wind. His hands were fisted deep in his pockets.

I reached out to punch his arm. "Are you like a genius?"

264

"Maybe." A sliver of slyness curved a corner of his mouth.

"Well, at least you're more fun as a know-it-all than the Gloomy Gus like you've been being."

"You're one to talk."

Georgie and I set out tramping through the dried hollyhocks and grasses.

"Carmen?"

I turned back to Jimmy.

"I was wondering," he said, frowning at me. "Are you ever afraid? I mean, do you worry if we start being the way we used to be—not sad all the time? More normal-like? That it will be like we're forgetting about Mom?"

Georgie looked up to see what my answer would be. Because it was a good question.

"Yeah." I shivered in the cold wind. "But if Mom is watching over us, and she is, I think she'd be unhappy to look down from heaven and see us being sad for-ever, don't you imagine?"

Jimmy nodded, then he tugged at the outhouse door. "She'd be surprised to look down and find us here, I'll bet."

Georgie and I petted Gertie, who seemed awfully

happy to have company for the holidays. Afterward Clark and the twins ran ahead of us to the top of the hill behind the house. They turned somersaults in the chilly wind and dry grass. They lay down flat and rolled themselves like pencils down the hill, making themselves dizzy, but Georgie held tight to my hand. He used his other hand to point at a noisy crow, then a long V of geese. After they disappeared in the high clouds, we could still hear them honking to each other.

I searched the sky and found a patch of the palest blue. I wondered, Are you up there, Mama? Boy, how I'd love to call you up and hear what you'd say about this, about us being here like this, because anyway, I can't remember the sound of your voice. It's like you're already fading. It's as if every day we live, we're leaving you farther behind, like we're turning our backs on you, like we didn't care—but we do, Mama. We really do, but now Dad's falling apart.

If only I could hand that magic phone to him. Mama would know how to help Dad be steady.

I had to think of something.

Did he really think that Robin's mom could break up our family worse than we already were? Would she try? "That'll be the day," I muttered. We might be a bizwang, messed-up family, but we were mine. Georgie was holding my hand tightly. "Come on, kiddo, we'd better go back inside. It's cold out here!"

"Look," he said, pointing a chubby finger at our station wagon. Jimmy was sitting in the driver's seat.

"Let's go see where Jimmy's going," I said. "Maybe he'll take us home, huh?"

"Yeah."

Jimmy was frowning out the windshield, stretching to touch the pedals with the toes of his tennis shoes as he turned the steering wheel this way and that.

"I'm really worried about Dad," he said, keeping his eyes on his imaginary road.

"Well, yeah."

"Darn you, Carmen, why did you have to stay next door all that time? What were you doing over there anyway?" He scowled at me and picked at the bandage on his burnt finger.

"I said I was sorry a million times, and why didn't you keep an eye on things like I asked you?"

Jimmy gave the inside of the car door a gloomy sort of kick and changed the subject. "We gotta go home.

Do you think you could drive this thing?"

That'd give Walter Cronkite some news: me at the wheel, Dad in the back with the baby and the boys. Dad came out on the broken-down porch. "What are you kids doing out there?" He pointed to his wristwatch. "This thing says it's lunchtime."

We bowed our heads and closed our eyes so Dad could say grace for our Thanksgiving dinner of baloney sandwiches, cider, and oranges. Through a curtain of eyelashes, I saw Dad's folded hands tremble and a muscle twitch in his red-stubbled cheek as Velvet went on babytalking to herself.

"Dear Father in Heaven, I want to thank you for Velvet, Georgie, Harry, Larry, Clark, Jimmy, Carmen, and please tell their mother, there with you in heaven, that . . . that we all miss her."

We stole glances when Daddy paused. Clark bit his lip.

"Thank you, Lord, for getting us here safe, sound, and all together. We humbly ask your help in keeping us that way and we sure thank you for this Thanksgiving dinner. Amen." Dad looked at us, and tears glittered in his red-rimmed eyes. He cleared his throat and said,

"Now all of you say Amen too."

"Amen."

Daddy gave Velvet her bottle. "Now eat up, everybody. And Carmen, I'll thank you and Jimmy to quit looking at me like I've snapped my cap and lost every marble in my head. Sit up and eat your lunch."

"Aunt Bevy was going to make us a turkey," said Clark. "I'll bet she's really worried about us." He talked the way people talk to kidnappers on TV.

Dad bowed his head and covered his eyes with the hand he wasn't using to hold Velvet's bottle. He muttered, "Bevy knows enough to know that if you all are with me, you're just fine. You all worry too much."

Then he looked up and squared his shoulders. His voice and his eyes went hard. "You know, I didn't go off to war and fight for no government that would up and take a man's children away from him."

Clark's eyes widened over the edge of his paper cup of cider. Jimmy and I exchanged alarmed glances.

"That woman's a schoolteacher." Dad bit out the words. "The authorities—the social workers, like she said—they'll listen to her!"

"But Dad, Robin's mom was probably upset about

stuff that had nothing to do with us and she just got carried away. And that fire could happen to anybody!" I cried.

"And this isn't even our house anymore, Daddy."

"Don't argue with me, Harry, or any of you." Dad's voice was tired and soft again. "I know we can't stay here. I just had to, you know, get away from there, from that hard-luck joint."

"But Dad," I burst out, "*we're* the part of the house that's in trouble!"

"Yeah, Dad," Clark put in. "And this place doesn't look very lucky, either." He waved his hand in the direction of the drafty, spidery old rooms.

"Besides, at home we have friends."

"And," Jimmy's voice was even and mild, "if we stay here and you get fired and we miss a bunch of school, then people really will think you can't take care of us." Through his thick, slippy glasses, he returned Dad's stony stare, flint for squint. "Maybe we can find us a grown-up to help Carmen cook and look after us. I'll get a paper route or something to help pay."

Dad was in no mood for reasonableness. He rolled right over our arguments. "You kids are too young to look after yourselves. Your Aunt Bevy has all she can do to manage her own life, getting her outfits to match her toenail polish. I just don't see how we can live without . . ." Dad bowed his head again, and Clark put his arms around him. "That battle-ax was right. I haven't been taking good care of you—not while I've had to earn a living at the same time. We may just have to make some adjustments, that's all."

"But Dad," I interrupted.

Slowly Dad stood and handed Velvet to me so he could go look out the window in the front door. "We have to cut our coat to fit the cloth. Maybe . . ." His voice trailed off, and he wrapped his big hand around the china doorknob.

"Aren't you going to even eat dinner?" I asked.

"I'm not hungry. I'm just going to go for a little walk. Don't you kids worry so much, for crying out loud." He pulled the door shut, and even Velvet watched him go past the window and out into the yard. What the heck were we going to do? If Dad was as hopeless as he looked, us Cathcarts really *were* doomed.

Clark slid down in his chair and frowned across the table at me. "How come Darren's mom's so mad about us being by ourselves anyway, Carmen? We were doing okay enough." Then he lowered his eyes kind of shifty-like and mumbled, "Until those stupid pies caught on fire."

Before I could say anything, Harry piped up, "If only Daddy didn't have to go to work."

"Yeah," Larry interrupted. "He has to go away before we even get home from school."

Georgie frowned over the top of his cup. He lowered it and wiped the back of his hand across his mouth and said, "He needs to stay home with us!"

I cocked my head to one side and looked at my baby brother. "Boy, for a dopey little kid, that's a pretty good idea!"

"I'm not dopey!"

"If Dad could do his job when we were at school," I said, "we could be together at night."

"But," Jimmy asked, "what about Georgie and the baby? In the daytime?"

"Well, what if . . . ?" I took a bite of my sandwich and tried to think of a way to fix things.

"I like Mr. Herman," said Georgie. "He gives me candy."

Clark rolled his eyes. "So?"

"So," I said, "maybe Georgie's the real genius of the family." Georgie's dirty face brightened up as he stuck his tongue out at Clark. "We'll ask Mr. Herman and the Monroe ladies and anybody else we can think of if they can help us find people to take turns babysitting while Dad's at work in the daytime." Harry and Larry traded glances, then nodded at me. We'd make adjustments, like Dad said, like giving up Art class. I clenched my jaw, flipped a towel onto my shoulder, and picked up the baby.

"Let's go talk to Daddy," said Clark.

"Yeah," I agreed as I patted Velvet's back.

"Maybe then," Jimmy added, "we can get away from this rotten little house on the prairie."

Velvet *brrupp*ed. Giggling brothers surrounded us, tucking in their chins, swallowing, and broadcasting fine burps of their own.

"Watch 'em, Georgie. This is something big boys gotta know," I said, gathering up Velvet's blankets. "Come on, you guys. Finish eating, then get your coats. Let's go tell Dad it's time to go home."

Outside, brown leaves whirled around us in frosty gusts of air. We heard rackety crows and blue jays as we crunched through dry leaves and weeds, me with the baby, Jimmy carrying Georgie piggyback, squinting our eyes against the windy light, looking for Dad.

"There he is!" Larry called out.

I watched Larry, Jimmy, and Georgie, following after Harry and Clark, speeding toward Dad and calling to him. I saw Dad, up on the crest of the hill, turn and stretch out his arms to the boys, and it was the weirdest thing. I was standing there, beside the old house, letting it protect Velvet and me from the wind, and I looked up at my family, what was left of it. And it sort of seemed like I was seeing them for the first time. There they all were, silhouetted against the clear sky over Blue Top.

I liked them.

Seventeen

*In which Thanksgiving is no baloney, we return
to the scene of the flaming pies, and Mr. Beeler has a surprise.*

All my brothers straggled down the hill, Georgie riding high on Dad's shoulders. "Did you guys tell him our plan?" I shouted. "Can we go home?"

"Yeah, we did," Jimmy hollered.

Clark cupped his hands around his mouth. "He said okay!"

"Seems to me," Dad called out, "the real question's what the heck are you doin' out in this cold with that baby girl?" As he came closer, I could see he wasn't mad, just real tired looking. "Now don't just be standin' there, Carmie, gawkin' at me that way. Let's go on in the house, then yeah, sure, I reckon we'd better get on home." We took hold of each other's hands. "Lemme grab a bite to eat first," he said as he followed Velvet and me into the house. "That okay?"

I smiled at him.

"Sure, Dad."

He wolfed down a pair of sandwiches. "Jimmy," he said, with his mouth full, "you and Clark be gettin' stuff together. Harry, you and Larry help 'em load up the car." He pushed his ball cap to the back of his head, then dug his thumbnails into the peel of an orange as he smiled a tired smile at Georgie.

"Did you think of this here babysitting plan all by yourself?"

Georgie nodded, looking real serious. He tore at his floppy baloney with his tiny teeth.

"Well." Dad shared out orange sections. "Well," he said again, shaking his head.

"We'll figure things out." I shrugged a shoulder. "As long as, well, you know, we're all still together."

Dad turned up one side of his mouth. "You're a philosopher, Buddy." He got to his feet, kissed and ruffled the top of my head, and messed up my hair even worse than it was. "Well, come on then. Let's hit the road before that wildcat Culpepper dame sends the coppers out after us."

"Oh Dad," I started to tell him, "she wouldn't—"

"Hey, wait—!" said Clark, and I heard it too: an engine. Then tires on gravel.

"Daddy," Harry called to us from the porch, "I think there's somebody coming!"

"Carmen," said Jimmy. "Look!"

Another shocker! "What's she doing here?" I cried.

The second her dust-covered Volkswagen ground to a stop, Aunt Bevy jumped out and began hugging everybody.

"How'd you find us?" I asked.

"Oh, feminine intuition," said Aunt Bevy. "I knew your old man had a soft spot for this place—heaven knows why!" She shot a worried smile at my dad.

He lifted his ball cap and one of his eyebrows at her. "Happy Thanksgiving to you, Beverly. It ain't much warmer inside, but let's get in out of this wind and you can tell us what you're doing here."

"What am *I* doing here!" Aunt Bevy marched herself up the porch steps and put one of her gloved hands on Dad's cheek. On the other side of his face, she made an orange smooch-print. "Now, Gene, what's the deal?"

Dad held the door open for her. "Come on in, Bev."

She kept talking as we all trooped indoors. "Frank and I lugged a big bird and all the trimmings over to your house this morning and you could have knocked all three of us over with a feather when we saw your smoky old house stinking like burnt pie and nobody home!"

"Where's Mr. Beeler?" I asked. "How come he didn't come with you?"

"Honey, he and the turkey are at my place. He's cooking so everything'll be done by the time I get you home! Did I tell you he's a whizbang in the kitchen?"

Dad and I widened our eyes at each other as Jimmy exclaimed, "We were just now going back home!"

Aunt Bevy frowned at our surroundings. "I'll say you are!"

"Where's your dog?" Georgie asked.

"Oh, Trixie's home reading the funnies. Carmen—?" Aunt Bevy's hoarse voice shifted into goo-goo gear: "Hand me that little girl baby! Now," she said, taking hold of Velvet, "what the heck happened? I want the whole story!"

"Carmen was next door." Jimmy spilled out the full report, clear down to his burnt finger and Mrs. Culpepper's blowing her stack. "She said Dad couldn't take care of us."

Aunt Bevy looked shocked.

"And Darren's mom said we should be in an orphanage," Clark supplied the big finish. "Or something like that."

"Eu-gene Cathcart!" Aunt Bevy exclaimed. "That hussy did not say that, did she?"

Daddy twitched his shoulders in a sad sort of shrug.

"Well, I'll be a beefsteak tomato! Robin told me there'd been a fire and a terrible ruckus, then you all took off like scalded cats, but her mom called her inside before I heard the whole lowdown."

"It was my fault, really," I said.

Aunt Bevy looked at me real concerned and kind, and she wrapped her gloved fingers around my hand. "I should have been there to help you. I'm sorry, Carmen."

"It was just those dumb pies," I said. "I made them and turned the oven to 375° like the recipe said."

A small voice said, "Uh-oh."

"Clark?" Dad said. "Do you know something about something?"

Clark looked like a rabbit whose name had just been called at the dentist. "I only wanted the pies to get done," he said in a voice we could hardly hear.

"Did you turn up the heat on the oven?" Jimmy asked. "You did, didn't you?"

"Just a little bit," Clark mumbled.

"How much of a little bit?" I demanded.

Clark looked away from me and held up five fingers.

"Five? Five hundred degrees!"

He nodded.

Yep. That'd get it done in a hurry. That'd be a story for his grandchildren: "Hooboy, that Grandpa Clark! Now he was a corker!"

"Still," said Dad, gripping my shoulder, "you are much to blame, Carmen, for going off and leaving those kids on their own."

"I know."

"Let's call it a lesson and leave it at that," he went on. "I reckon there's been enough punishment to go around."

"Well," said Aunt Bevy, "from the looks of things,

your house isn't in that bad of shape. You'll want some paint and—" She screamed.

"You never had a goat look at you through a window before," Clark asked, "huh, Aunt Bevy?"

"It's only Gertie," said Jimmy. "She's a Toggenburg goat, just for you to know."

It wasn't long after that that Aunt Bevy and Clark, who begged to ride with her, were churning up the gravel road behind us as we left Blue Top for the last time. Through our comet tails of dust, I saw the lonely farmhouse shrinking away. Was that how it was, I wondered. My imagination made one more way to think about Mama: us moving on down the road, Mama left behind, always mild and smiling, never older and always right there in the past where we left her, but fading and shrinking because we were going on into the future. We couldn't help it. That's what you do if you're alive.

I turned to look out the dusty windshield. In my lap, Velvet was happily kicking her legs. "I always thought I was so tough," Daddy murmured.

"You are, Dad."

He sighed. "You kids are the ones," he said.

* * *

After the long drive and sharing Thanksgiving supper with Aunt Bevy, Mr. Beeler, and Trixie, it was dark when we got back. So we didn't really see our house until the Friday morning sun climbed over the edge of the world. Poor old Cathcart Castle.

"Jeepers," I said, "it's sure gonna need a bunch of scrubbing and painting, huh, Dad?"

"Oh yeah, but shoot," he said, "I figure it needed that anyway."

"I'm glad it didn't burn down," said Jimmy. "Aren't you, Dad?"

"Yup, we can be thankful for that, son. We'll air it out, fix 'er up."

Aunt Bevy had filled her VW with lots of leftovers to eat. Mr. Beeler got buckets and paintbrushes out of the back of his Chevy, but the Culpeppers and their Buick weren't home. I sure hoped they were all okay. Even if a house was clean and tidy, that didn't mean that everything was dandy with the people who lived in it. I guess Robin's mom taught me that.

"Well, now!" said Miss Lillian. She and Miss Effie welcomed us home with plenty of smiles, hugs, and head pats. Nodding Mr. Herman pumped Dad's hand in a hard shake and passed out a handful of peppermints. "Now let's see if we can't help you straighten up this mess."

It was hard to drop Mama's ruined straw castle into the trash, but it'd be stupid, of course, to just stand and look at a wastebasket and feel bad. I opened the windows to let some cold, clean air into our house. I stuffed smoky clothes into the washing machine and real quick, before I went back up to help, it was nice to listen to everyone talking and thumping around up over my head.

By the time the sun went down, our spic-and-span downstairs smelled so much like Ajax and fresh paint, Mrs. Culpepper would probably want to move in with us. Mr. Beeler had gone to do some undertaker business. His bald head turned pink when Clark and me caught him kissing Aunt Bevy and saying, "Be back later, Sweetie." The Monroe ladies went home, telling Dad, "Have faith, Mr. Cathcart. Things are lookin' up around here." Velvet, in her baby seat, waved her arms and supervised while I helped Aunt Bevy fix food for everybody.

"Carmen? I was wondering, well . . . what do you think of Frank?"

"Mr. Beeler? You mean how he smooches you and

laughs at all your jokes? You wanna know if I think he's stuck on you?"

"Okay, yes, Miss Smarty."

"I *was* kind of wondering if you guys were in love or something." When Aunt Bevy smiled, sort of happy and mysterious, I asked her, "Is he as nice as Bill?"

Aunt Bevy pursed her lips. My asking about her long-ago first husband made her look at me for a minute, kind of wistful and tender-like. "He is," she said, turning back to her sandwich making.

"Do you think he's gonna ask you to marry him?"

"Well . . ." She carried a platter of turkey sandwiches into the dining room, her loud voice louder as she went on. "He might be a *bit* younger than I am. On the other hand, I'm afraid I *am* just an old nut who's fallen for Frank the Undertaker. He's just the sweetest, funniest, cutest freckle-headed man," she said, coming back into the kitchen. "Oh, what if he heard me talking all this mushy talk—wouldn't it be terrible? I think I'd faint!"

I smothered a smile at the sight of Aunt Bevy looking frozen and popeyed at the sight of Mr. Beeler, who'd just come in our back door.

"Where'd you come from?" she cried. "How long have you been standing there?"

"I just walked in," he said, smiling real innocent. "What do you mean? Did I miss something?" When she looked away, he winked at me. For someone who'd told such a whopper, he looked awfully happy. I liked Mr. Beeler even better.

On Monday morning Robin's long black braids danced like twin whips as she hurried down the steps. Mrs. Culpepper came out on the porch, her lips pressed tight together. "How are you and your family?" she asked, looking troubled, and cold without a coat on. "Are you all okay, Carmen?"

"Yes, ma'am. I guess so." I didn't mind so much, now, being asked that.

"I'm glad," said Robin's mom. "Truly, Carmen, I'm glad you're all safe and I am . . . ," she called after us. We were hurrying to get to school, but I stopped and turned to face her.

"I *was* worried about you and your brothers," she said, "and the baby. And the fire—I see you're getting your house fixed right up. I shouldn't have gotten so upset." She looked so flustered I almost was sorry for

285

her. "Accept my apology, Carmen," she said. "Please."

"It's okay. It *was* pretty terrible." Things weren't truly okay, but I knew Mom'd want me to let Mrs. Culpepper off the hook.

Robin and I walked fast, and all that had happened to each of us since the fire tumbled out of our mouths on clouds of breath smoke.

"My folks, they've been having lots of fights about different stuff," Robin said. "Anyway, they made up enough, for now, so they're not going to get a divorce or anything—yet, anyway." She shot me a lopsided frown: who'd ever understand grown-ups? "And Mom's been real nice to me. She even cried and said she was sorry for taking out her bad feelings on me. She said I was perfect and she really loved me—like she meant it, even." Robin rolled her eyes at me, but I could pretty much tell that her heart was more peaceful about her mom.

It got me wondering how my mom and I would be getting along now and how she wouldn't ever get to see how we were gonna turn out. Robin's voice broke into these sad thoughts. "I just think Mom's not a happy person and it's not about her having me for a daughter."

"But your mom's so lucky to have you—I mean, you're the best!"

We walked fast against the cold, hugging our books to our chests, Robin looking pleased, me feeling kind of wistful about Mom, hearing Robin trying to figure out her own. "So could you?" I asked. "Did you forgive her?"

"Maybe. I told her I did. And she said she wouldn't really call the cops on your family. She just gets so mad sometimes." Robin shrugged and shook her head.

We turned the corner onto Maple, almost to school. I felt kind of mad too. In fact, I felt pretty furious at Old Yeller Culpepper, getting my poor dad so upset. "She's pretty old to be having tantrums."

"Don't I know it," Robin said.

Then I told her the important news: about Aunt Bevy and Mr. Beeler.

"Jeepers!" Robin grinned. "If they got married, maybe we could be bridesmaids, huh?"

It was kind of a big fat relief to go back to normal life, to school with kids scrambling out of the yellow buses, milling around the door of the school, like it was an anthill. When I got to my locker, Jenny Moffat smiled at me for the first time. "Man oh man, you Cathcarts sure have yourself some luck. I heard about that fire over at your place. You all okay? You need anything?"

"Naah," I said, feeling kind of famous. "But that's nice of you to ask."

Greg Tuck passed me a note in Health class. He'd drawn a fire engine on it.

Some kids said your house caught on fire.
Did all your stuff get burned up?
I bet you could draw a neat picture with
flames and smoke.

I showed it to Robin on the way home. She snorted. "Boys are so immature." Later, when we could hear Velvet bawling before we even got to my house, Robin made a face. "Boy, she doesn't sound very happy."

"Talk about immature!" I said, hurrying across our yard and up the steps.

"I think she's got a tummy ache going," said Dad, pulling on his coat.

"Carmie, that wild woman next door brought over a chocolate cake this morning before she left for the grade school. She told me she was sorry, so I told her I was just as spun up as she was, leaving you kids alone all the time, and we were all going to do our best. Now I gotta get to work. Keep the doors locked and keep that pyromaniac Clark away from the stove! Get it? Pie-romaniac?" Dad winked at me and grabbed up his lunch box.

"Did you call up your boss?" I jiggled fussy, wriggling Velvet.

"Oh, that's another thing," said Dad. "Mr. Herman will look in on you tonight—what a sweet old guy he is."

I raised my voice. "Didja?"

It had been a long time since Dad had been so silly and annoying.

"Get her blanket and walk me to the car. Doesn't she want her pacifier? She wouldn't take it for me, either."

"Dad, you're being impossible."

"Come on, Georgie, give me a kiss. Daddy's gotta go to work."

"Dad!"

Velvet quieted down when Dad gave her a good-bye hug. Not until he was in the car and reaching out to squeeze my hand did he answer me. "Yeah, yeah, I

289

personally talked to the supervisor on the phone and he said he might have an opening on the day shift after the first of the year. So how's that? And I called the Monroe sisters and lemme tell you, those ladies had lots of babysitting advice. Step back now. Be careful this evening, honey. Love you."

"Love you, too."

Dad backed down the driveway, then stopped.

"Oh yeah, I almost forgot. Frank Beeler's going to call you later. Wants to ask you something."

"Me?"

Did he want Miss Lillian's recipe for Hungarian Meatballs? Christmas gift advice for Aunt Bevy? Maybe Mr. Beeler could give me advice on something special a totally broke kid like me could give a father for Christmas? I wondered what Mr. Beeler wanted to ask me all through supper, then, when the phone rang, every single one of the boys had to say hey to him before my turn came.

"May I invite myself and your Aunt Beverly over to your house on Saturday night?" he asked. "We'll bring the supper."

"Huh?"

"I don't want to put you all to any trouble. I've had—
I mean to say, there's someone I want you all to meet
and . . . uhm . . . well, anyway, would it be all right?"

"Sure. Who's coming?"

"That's a surprise." Mr. Beeler chuckled. "Shall you
expect us?"

Well, sure. We said our good-bye-for-nows and I
hung up the phone, mystified.

Eighteen

In which I make discoveries.

"Hey! This is the seventh of December," said Jimmy, looking at Robin and me over the top of the Saturday morning newspaper. "Do you guys know what that day is?"

"Eighteen days till Christmas?" Robin guessed. Jimmy shook his head, and I could tell that we'd given him a lot of satisfaction, not knowing something he knew.

"It's the day that'll live in infamy, when we got attacked at Pearl Harbor in Hawaii, on December 7,

1941. In World War Two. Just for you to know."

I told him thanks for the good information.

"You know what else? That kid I told you about—Wally Williams? He's coming over here to see me." Jimmy looked proud.

"Neato. What are you guys going to do?"

"Wally's got a chess set, and I got a book from the library. We're gonna teach each other how to play chess."

That's what they were doing, too, when I met the kid, a little guy with big ears and good manners. He jumped up when I went into Jimmy's room, just about toppling the chess board. He even stuck out his hand, so I shook it as Jimmy said, "This is Wally and this is Carmen, my sister. She draws real good."

Wow, he'd never said that before.

"Can you draw me?" Wally asked, sitting back down, lifting his chin so I could size up his face.

Huh? If I didn't count doodling in Math, I hadn't drawn anything since I was in Mrs. Montisano's class. And I'd sure as heck never drawn a real live human being sitting right in front of me.

"Sure she could!" Jimmy sounded like a movie-guy

saying how fast his horse can run, so it'd be mean to let him down in front of the first kid he ever got to come visit him.

Wally Williams sat as still as an owl on a tree branch. It was hard—and fun—to draw a curve then a circle with a black dot in it and try to make them look like his left eye. Then you have to make the other eye match. I drew his pug nose, his pursed-up lips, tried not to make his ears look like two jug handles, tore out the page, and showed it to the kid. All the laughing he'd been holding in popped out all over the place.

"Neat! Can I keep it? I'm gonna give it to my mom for Christmas."

"Hey, it looks like him!" Jimmy exclaimed. "Draw me now!"

"Car-men!" Dad hollered up the stairs. "Come help Georgie, will ya? I got my hands full with the baby!"

"Maybe later, okay?" I told Jimmy. "Good luck with the chess. Nice to meecha."

Jimmy and that Wally kid gave me an idea. All the time I was helping Dad clear up to when Mr. Beeler's car came around our corner, I thought about it. It gave me the shivers.

The boys blasted out of the house to greet Mr. Beeler.

"What's that on top of your car?" Larry asked.

"It's a Christmas tree, dummy!" Clark shouted as Harry wondered, "Who's that in the backseat?"

"You'll see!" said Mr. Beeler, hurrying to open doors for Aunt Bevy and a lady with short, sticking-up hair. At all of our puzzled, bashful faces, she beamed a toothy smile.

Jimmy nudged me. "Who's that?"

She looked kind of familiar. "Beats me," I said.

"I want you all to meet Frances here!" said Mr. Beeler. "Frances, these are the Cathcarts."

Aunt Bevy's smile was as bright as her cherry red hat and coat. "I'll bet you all didn't know that Frank here had a twin sister."

Both Mr. Beeler and his sister grinned, crinkling their identical brown eyes at us Cathcarts. Frances took three big steps, her right hand outstretched, up to Dad coming down the porch steps to meet her.

"Frances Beeler. Mighty pleased to meet you."

Unlike Aunt Bevy's, Miss Beeler's dark eyes had no makeup, only lots of laugh wrinkles. She reminded me of the girls at school who actually liked PE class.

"Gene Cathcart," Dad said. "Pleasure's mine, Miss Beeler."

"And this must be Velvet." Her voice went higher. "What a pretty girl! Who's a pretty girl?" Miss Beeler jiggled Velvet's bootied foot.

When her brother opened the trunk of his car, barbecue smell spilled out. The boys helped unload cartons of Pepsi, strawberry pop, and greasy brown paper sacks.

"Let's everybody come inside," Dad called out. "Bev, do I have you to thank for that Christmas tree?"

"No, that was Frank's idea. Wasn't that sweet of him?"

"Yup," Dad agreed. "That was awful sweet, Frank, no foolin'!"

"Mr. Beeler, that lady's really your twin?" Jimmy asked.

"How come we never met her before?"

Mr Beeler looked real delighted that I'd asked him that. "Because she's been in Africa for the past two years!"

"Wow!" Jimmy looked amazed. "Where in Africa?"

"Go on in and ask her," said Mr. Beeler. "She'll tell you all about it."

"Wow," said Jimmy, softer this time. He hurried into the house, but not me and Mr. Beeler. We lollygagged behind, out on the front porch.

"Is your sister your big surprise?"

"Well, sure!" said Mr. Beeler. Curiosity sent his eyebrows clear up to the brim of his black fedora. "What'd you think it was?"

I tilted my head up at him. Like they do sometimes, words bubbled up out of nowhere and—okay, they came from my hoping—right up and out of my mouth.

"I kind of wondered, after you heard what Aunt Bevy said the other day, if you might ask her to marry you."

"How did—? I was going to—I mean, I *am*. Do you think she really wants me to?" He turned his face toward the bright indoors, where Aunt Bevy was laughing.

"Well, I did want to talk to you, Carmen, you and your father, and the rest of you, because . . . well, so little time has gone by since your mother passed away. . . ."

"It's okay, Mr. Beeler." I put my hand on his woolen sleeve to stop him. "It really is. Honest."

"Carmen!" Dad called from inside. "What in the Sam Hill are you two doin' out there? Come in and get some supper before we eat it all!"

I pulled Mr. Beeler's sleeve for him to lower his head. I said what I knew was true into his ear, "My mom would really like you, if she'd met you. I know she would. And well . . ." I frowned, trying to think how to say just what I meant. "I think our family would be a lot less busted if you were part of it."

His smile sort of melted at the edges. His dark eyes glittered as he draped an arm around my shoulder.

"Ask her tonight, why doncha?"

"No. Christmas!" he whispered, as he opened the door for me. "You know—more romantic! Don't tell her!"

I was glad I didn't have to say I wouldn't tell Robin about this. I hugged the exciting secret to myself as Mr. Beeler smooched Aunt Bevy's rouged cheek. My eyes were full of the sight of my family, Miss Beeler steadying Velvet's bottle with one hand, waving a drumstick with the other. My nose was full of supper smells, my mind was buzzing with the idea I got from drawing Wally. My heart was stuffed full of—oh, I don't know. What's really happy? Fizzy bluebirds?

"I'd been a nurse for years," Miss Beeler was saying, "but when President Kennedy, God rest him, started the Peace Corps, I knew I had my marching orders! I worked with the Pygmy women and their babies over in Gabon, on Africa's west coast. That's where Dr. Albert Schweitzer built his hospital, you know."

"Who's that?" Clark asked.

"He's a famous musician-doctor-writer fella," said Dad. "He won that big prize."

Miss Beeler nodded. "The Nobel Peace Prize."

"Did you see monkeys?" Harry asked.

"Hundreds of them!"

"Did you get to meet President Kennedy?" Jimmy asked.

"Shook hands with him," said Miss Beeler, and Jimmy gazed respectfully at her calloused right hand.

When everybody was full and licking their fingers, Dad helped bring in the tree from the top of Mr. Beeler's Chevy. It smelled green and wintery, like Christmas.

Larry turned to me. "Where are all our ornaments?"

"And our lights?" Harry added.

"They must be upstairs in your room," I said, "right, Dad?"

Dad nodded. "I think your mother stuck 'em in the closet."

As I went upstairs, I thought about my idea for a really special present for Dad. It'd be the best, hardest picture ever—if I had time. "If I could really do it," I said to myself as I felt for the light switch in my folks' room. *Click:* there was their big, empty bed. There in the closet were Mama's dresses. My face brushed against them as I searched through old boxes and bulging brown paper sacks for the decorations. I breathed in Mama's scents of baby powder and graham crackers and felt a little bit like crying. Inside a squashed sack, I found a bundle of old Christmas cards and our electric window candles. Underneath were all our ornaments. Some were store-bought, but mostly we made 'em: tinfoil stars, pipe-cleaner candy canes. What would we make this year? Snowflakes? I imagined Mama's spirit watching us glue glitter on construction paper angels, her being up there with bunches of real ones, her first Christmas in heaven. Then, under a tangle of tinsel, I saw something blue.

It was a package, wrapped in blue tissue paper. Bending closer, hardly breathing, I read the writing on it.

Happy Birthday, Carmen, love from Mama

I remembered when I stayed up late with Mama, that hot night before I turned thirteen, that last night. I could almost hear her telling me, "I saved an extra present, one your daddy doesn't know about yet, for Saturday, when we have your cake and candles."

Tears stung my nose, pushed against the backs of my eyes, and I let them come on out and roll down my cheeks. I heard Jimmy's faraway voice calling me.

"Whatcha doin'? Didja find the ornaments?"

My tears dripped on my hands tearing at the paper, careful to save the part with Mama's writing. You know what was inside? A paintbox. A wooden box with two brushes and a set of watercolors.

I heard Dad on the stairs. "Carmen? You okay up there?"

The paints were in little tubes. Like real artists use. It was like she was giving me permission to have my castle in the air, the way Mr. Herman talked about it: a dream of what I could be. It was almost like Mama was *counting* on me to be a real artist someday.

Boy, I really started bawling. I still was when Daddy came up and found me. I showed him the paints and, between sobs, I told him what they meant.

"She was proud of me."

"We both were!" he said, pretty weepy himself. "My gosh, Buddy, I never was so proud of anybody as I am of you."

The very next day, I drew a picture of Jimmy, remembering how Mrs. Montisano told us to measure what we were trying to draw, getting both sides of his glasses to match, all the while his eyes staring right at me. I told him my big idea for Dad's Christmas present.

Jimmy smiled really big, and I had to stop drawing. A smile squinches up the eyes, and teeth are too hard to draw. "Wow! Carmen, that's so excellent. Dad will like that better than anything! But will he be in it?"

Wow, that was a neat idea except for one problem. "He can't sit and be looking at me while I draw him. It'd wreck the surprise."

"What if you looked at a picture of him in the photo album," Jimmy suggested.

Now I was smiling. "You really *are* a genius."

Beside him, on the same piece of paper, I drew Clark.

"Don't make me look stupid," he said.

"If I do, I promise it won't be on purpose."

I had to look at myself in the mirror, it seemed like forever, to draw my own picture. After school on Monday, I drew Georgie and about erased a hole in the paper, he moved around so much. Being busy made me wait before I could draw Harry, then Larry, then, when she was asleep, baby Velvet. I drew her in front of Dad with his arms holding her. Last of all, I made Mama's face, calm and mild, the way she looked in the picture of her in my billfold, from when we were at Blue Top, the way she always looked in my mind. With a brush and a teeny bit from the tube labeled Cerulean Blue, I carefully, carefully, painted blue sky behind us Cathcarts and around Mama. She rested her elbows on a puffy cloud above us all. I gave her wings.

I'd imagine all of the passed-on people. President Kennedy and his baby boy, the Alabama Sunday school girls, all of the flowing-robed angels and those piggy-looking, fairy-winged baby angels, plus the old gods and goddesses. God and Jesus and Mama, all watching from their blue-cloud kingdoms or green pastures or golden cities, all gazing down on the world of Christmas Eve, 1963.

If they looked into our town, would they see and hear Mr. Scudder sitting by himself, holding a bent postcard from some army base, staring at his television, not seeing either one? Miss Effie and Miss Lucille and Mr. Herman sharing cocoa and a Christmas cake? Wondering what's inside the presents they got from those Cathcarts? Robin's dad playing "Silent Night" on his piano and singing at the deep end of his family quartet? My slick-haired brothers with red bow ties clipped to their collars and giggles twitching the corners of their mouths?

They'd for sure see Dad admiring Velvet's foofy baby dress from Aunt Bevy's department store. Jolly Miss Beeler spraying crumbs, talking around bites of Christmas cookie. Nervous Mr. Beeler looking at Aunt Bevy and checking, when he didn't think anybody saw, if he still had the tiny ring box in his pocket. Aunt Bevy crying, "Ta-da!" and shaking out a brand-new dream castle in the air for our *Sputnik* chandelier.

"Carmie," Clark whispered, "when you gonna give him the present?"

"Now." He helped me pull it out from behind our old couch. It was big and heavy, too, because Aunt Bevy got a real picture frame, with glass.

"This is for you, Dad," I said.

He looked at me real hard and bright and tore off the tissue paper. Dad looked at my picture the way he looked at Velvet sometimes. Tears came in his eyes and in almost everybody else's when they clustered around Dad looking at the drawing I did.

"There we all are," he said softly.

"I made Mama our guardian angel," I told him. I made her like in my imagination, smiling down from heaven at us Cathcarts, all festive and bittersweet.

And then . . .

After the turn of the year, Dad's job did change. In the evenings, there he would be, with us. And in the daytime, when Georgie and baby Velvet needed looking after, our friends, their friends, plus the nursery school Robin's mom helped us find, all helped us to live our momless life.

At last, at last, the Last Day of School came at last, and did I survive eighth grade? Well, sure. My mom didn't raise any stupid kids.

On the last weekend in May, in the very back of our old station wagon, Larry was teaching Georgie how to play Old Maid. In the middle seat, Harry and Clark each held canning jars, wrapped in old *Examiners*, full of pink and white peonies. They craned their necks, trying to count the cows in the fields we passed on our way to the graveyard. In the front seat, Dad drove with one hand on the wheel, the other out the window so the highway wind could blow across his tattooed angel harp. I held the baby. Velvet's toes pressed into my lap as she stood on her sturdy, rubbery legs. She swiveled her head to smile slobbery smiles at whichever boy called her name.

"She's wanting to be walking," said Dad. "And her only ten months old."

As soon as Dad parked the station wagon near the cars of the other Decoration Day visitors, the little boys bubbled out the doors. Jimmy followed more slowly, his finger marking the place in his book. Velvet struggled in my arms, so I set her down in the bright, thick grass. Around the old cemetery, people turned their heads at the sound of her happy shrieks. The twins balanced the peony jars on the grass beside the stones that marked Mama's and her long-gone folks' resting places.

I pulled the elastic that held my ponytail so my red hair could blow free. The wind smelled like rain.

Boiling ivory, pearly cloud mountains floated in the deepest blue of the sky over us, the graveyard, the sleepers under the stones, the trees, and the river. For a moment I let myself imagine floaty-gowned, long-haired goddesses and angels up there, like in the paintings of the mythological lands, in the art books in the library. Then I asked Dad something I'd been wondering.

"Do you forget sometimes how Mom's voice sounded?"

"Naah, Buddy," said Dad, and he kissed the top of my head. "I remember it okay. I just listen to you."

Velvet's fat baby fingers gripped the edge of Mama's tombstone. She pulled herself up and, after a moment, she let go and stood wobbling and balancing in the springy grass.

"Look, Daddy!" Larry called. "Velvet's walking!"

Cheryl Harness lives in Independence, Missouri, with her Scottie, Maude, and two cats, MerrieEmma and Elizabeth. As an author and illustrator, she is known for her engaging approach to history, seen in such books as THREE YOUNG PILGRIMS, GHOSTS OF THE WHITE HOUSE, and REMEMBER THE LADIES. JUST FOR YOU TO KNOW is her first novel.